CHAIN REACTION

TWENTIETH CENTURY FOX PRESENTS A ZANUCK COMPANY / CHICAGO PACIFIC ENTERTAINMENT / KIRLE LEONARD PRODUCTION AN ANDREW DAVIS FILM

KEANU REEVES MORGAN FREEMAN "CHAIN REACTION" RACHEL WEISZ FRED WARD KEVIN DUNN BRIAN COX

MUSIC JERRY GOLDSMITH
BY JERRY GOLDSMITH

FILM DONALD DUDLEY DON BRUCE A.C.E. ARTHUR SCHMIDT
EDITORS DONALD DUDLEY DON BRUCE A.C.E. ARTHUR SCHMIDT

PRODUCTION MAHER AHMAD
DESIGNER MAHER AHMAD

DIRECTOR OF FRANK TIDY B.S.C.
PHOTOGRAPHY FRANK TIDY B.S.C.

EXECUTIVE RICHARD D ZANUCK CHARLES SEWELL
PRODUCERS RICHARD D ZANUCK CHARLES SEWELL

SCREENPLAY JOSH FRIEDMAN AND J.F. LAWTON AND MICHAEL BORTMAN
BY JOSH FRIEDMAN AND J.F. LAWTON AND MICHAEL BORTMAN

STORY ARNE L. SCHMIDT & RICK SELTZER AND JOSH FRIEDMAN
BY ARNE L. SCHMIDT & RICK SELTZER AND JOSH FRIEDMAN

PRODUCED ARNE L. SCHMIDT ANDREW DAVIS
BY ARNE L. SCHMIDT ANDREW DAVIS

DIRECTED ANDREW DAVIS
BY ANDREW DAVIS

20th CENTURY FOX
© 1996 TWENTIETH CENTURY FOX

DOLBY
IN SELECTED THEATRES

Soundtrack Available on VARÈSE RECORDS
VARÈSE SARABANDE

CHAIN REACTION

A NOVEL BY ROBERT TINE
SCREENPLAY BY JOSH FRIEDMAN AND J.F. LAWTON AND MICHAEL BORTMAN
STORY BY ARNE L. SCHMIDT & RICK SEAMAN AND JOSH FRIEDMAN

St. Martin's Paperbacks

CHAIN REACTION

TM and copyright © 1996 by Twentieth Century Fox Film Corporation. All rights reserved.

Cover photograph by Deana Newcomb.

ISBN: 0-312-95884-6

Printed in the United States of America

St. Martin's Paperbacks edition/August 1996

10 9 8 7 6 5 4 3 2 1

CHAIN REACTION

CHAPTER ONE

"We have reached a new stage in the history of mankind!"

Professor Bucholtz paused dramatically, his eyes glittering as he scanned the faces of the 300 or so rapt students who had packed Mandle Hall that morning. He had been speaking for twenty minutes, and so far no one had moved a muscle, no one had made a sound. The professor was nothing if not a showman. On a table in front of the speaker's podium was an exhibit of some kind, hidden from the audience, covered by a sheet. There was no doubt that at the most dramatic moment possible, Professor Bucholtz would remove the cloth like a magician unveiling a particularly fiendish bit of hocus-pocus.

He waited until the echo of his words had died away, the sound of the city of Chicago worming its way back into the cavernous lecture hall, then began to speak again. The professor spoke softly at first, the offhand, almost conversational tone of his voice at odds with the weightiness of his subject.

"A new stage," Bucholtz repeated, "in which the limits of the past can simply be discarded as nothing more than old and now irrelevant ways of thinking."

From the podium Professor Bucholtz could see frowns and smiles as well as puzzled looks on the faces of his audience. The frowns came from students who were not pleased to be told that so much of what they had learned so diligently, so tirelessly, was about to become as obsolete as a steam engine or a stagecoach; the smiles came from those who welcomed new things simply because they were fresh, reveling in the current and the up-to-date because they liked to think of themselves on the cutting edge, condemning the old way. The puzzled looks were the ones Professor Bucholtz welcomed. These were the people who were thinking hard about what he was saying, reflecting seriously on each and every word he uttered.

"We are within sight of an age-old dream of mankind. We will soon have the capacity for all peoples in all nations to extinguish poverty," the professor continued, his voice rising again. "Simply snuff it out, the way we've conquered smallpox or polio. And what is the source of this new wealth?"

Almost as one, the audience leaned forward as if only a lucky few would hear the answer to the professor's rhetorical question.

But Bucholtz did not speak. Instead, he reached for the glass and the carafe of water on the podium and poured until the glass was filled to the brim. He lifted it, examined it, then put the glass to his lips and drank about half of the water in a single draught.

Stepping away from the podium he drew the cloth from his exhibit, revealing a small, working model of the experiment that he and his staff were engaged with. There were two stainless steel holding tanks connected with copper tubing to a glass distillation vial sitting on a glowing gas ring. Bucholtz poured the rest of the water in the glass into the apparatus and then glanced at the audience. There was an amused twinkle in his dark eyes.

"Water," he said. "H_2O . . . A compound you have all been familiar with since your very first day in chemistry class. It consists of two parts hydrogen and one part oxygen. And it is, as you know, a rather simple matter to separate the compound into its component parts."

As he spoke, the water divided into hydrogen and oxygen funneling into separate holding tanks, bubbling softly.

"We've done it here," Professor Bucholtz said, indicating the people in the front row of the auditorium. "We" in the professor's parlance being the members of his team who sat in the places of honor smiling broadly.

Bucholtz's close-knit crew was a veritable United Nations of researchers, scientists the professor had culled from a half a dozen countries around the world: there was a young chemist from China, a physicist from the Czech Republic, a Frenchman, a South African, as well as a number of Americans.

Not sitting with the scientists but roosted high up in the uppermost tier of the lecture hall was Eddie Kasalivich, Chicago born and bred. He hung on the professor's every word, scarcely breathing as Bucholtz spoke.

"The division of water into its component parts is quite simple," the professor continued. "We've done it here." He gestured towards the apparatus on the table in front of him.

"But here's the rub: the energy required to make the split, as we say, is greater than the energy we derive from the separated parts. But let us see the power of the energy we have created."

Bucholtz turned a small brass valve—a valve that Eddie Kasalivich had himself machined—opening the hydrogen tank, the gas escaping with a soft hiss. The professor struck a match and lit it, the gas igniting with a boom, a small explosion followed by a clear blue flame. The audience tittered nervously. Bucholtz's eyes flashed, and he smiled slyly at his listeners.

"It is, after all, the same power that reduced the famous zeppelin, the *Hindenburg*, to a smoking ruin in a matter of seconds. But what happens when we have learned how to separate those same elements in a way that requires very little energy?"

It was an interesting question but in a purely theoretical way. Every first-year physics student knew that the division of hydrogen and oxygen would always require more energy than it produced. Still, it was fun to speculate . . .

"I will give you the answer to my own question," said Bucholtz. "And it is a simple one . . . If we were able to do this, we would transform the world. Think of it: we will have found a way to make fire from water. We will have an inexhaustible resource. For water is everywhere, and it doesn't matter if it's clean or dirty, salty or fresh." He paused again as the audience thought about a world that would be powered by water rather than expensive oil or dirty coal.

"And here's the truly exciting part," said Bucholtz. "It's a completely nonpolluting resource as well. For what happens when you burn hydrogen? You get a waste product that is . . . water."

The professor picked up his glass of water and sipped, the audience chuckling appreciatively.

"We put an end to pollution," he said, his voice rising in intensity. "We put an end to our eternal fight for limited resources. All of a sudden, there's enough to go around, enough for every nation. Maybe we start to put an end to war, to the endless geopolitical struggles . . ."

Upstairs in the last row in the balcony James Shannon slipped into the seat next to Eddie.

"You're late," Eddie whispered to the older man.

Shannon seemed unconcerned. "I love The Speech," he said. "I've heard it a hundred times before."

In the rarefied realms of particle physics Professor Franklin "Bucky" Bucholtz was famous for a number of things: his unorthodox, arcane discoveries in out-of-the-way corners of a difficult discipline, a degree of absentmindedness, a keen sense of humor. But best of all, he was known for this, The Speech. The vision of a better, cleaner world. A world he had created in his own mind and which he had decided to try to make a reality as well.

"The only way to change this world is to change the way we handle technology," Bucholtz declared passionately. "This planet cannot survive the waste of another industrial revolution. The chance to save our planet and our place on it may be at our fingertips. We cannot let it slip away. We don't have the time." His voice rang to the rafters of the stately old hall.

Professor Bucholtz paused and then shrugged lightly, a slight gesture of self-deprecation. "Of course, we have to make it work first."

The audience laughed. The applause was loud and sustained.

CHAPTER TWO

Deep in the industrial crust that surrounded Chicago, the landscape of old mills and rusting train tracks stood as a reminder of the spirit of industrial enterprise that had once flourished here. The plants and factories were, for the most part, silent and still now, but one old works was as busy as it had been in the glory days of American industrial might. This was the home to Professor Bucholtz and the team members of the undertaking that the professor had dubbed the Bessemer Project. Few people on or off the team had noticed the irony of the name—Sir Henry Bessemer, inventor of the process that bore his name, was a nineteenth-century scientist who had done much to advance the course of the wasteful Industrial Revolution that Bucky Bucholtz deplored so deeply.

The old mill was a hive of activity. There were fifteen or twenty research workers scattered around the huge space, each working on a small part of a giant equation. The only person actually laboring on the machine was Lu Chen, a young scientist from Shanghai, China. He was bent over a far larger version of the demonstration apparatus the professor had shown off at his lecture and was carefully putting a stainless steel assembly into place in the middle of the contraption, looking up as Eddie Kasalivich walked quickly into the lab.

He waved and smiled, then turned his attention back to the steel assembly, settling the huge piece of steel delicately on its mounting points.

"Hey, Eddie," Lu called. "Got a space right here." He pointed to an empty coupling in the middle of the frame. "Have to have it fill."

" 'Filled,' Chen," said Eddie, laughing. "That's 'filled' . . . And I'm working on it, okay? Get off my back."

The professor was hunched over a vast set of blueprints covering his desk from edge to edge. Beside him was his chief staff scientist, a brainy, beautiful and, to Eddie, rather scary young woman named Lily Sinclair. She was bent over the blueprints as well, explaining something to Professor Bucholtz

When Eddie burst into Bucholtz's office, it was Sinclair who looked up sharply, annoyed at the interruption.

"Don't bother to knock or anything," said Sinclair peevishly.

Kasalivich's lack of manners plainly did not bother the professor. "What's up, Eddie?"

Eddie tore open his backpack and extracted a conical-shaped piece of steel and held it up like a trophy from the winning game.

"Six microns," he said. "I worked it down to only six microns." He pointed to the sharp-pointed tip on the end of the cone.

Bucholtz did an exaggerated double take. "Six?" He slipped his glasses down from his forehead and reached for the nozzle.

"You got a consistent droplet size of six microns?"

Eddie nodded and looked triumphant. "Yeah." He noted with a certain satisfaction that even Lily Sinclair looked impressed at his achievement.

"But how did you do it?" the professor asked,

peering at the finely worked piece of steel.

Eddie laughed. "I have absolutely no idea!"

"Well, let's see if it works . . . "

Chen screwed the nozzle into the coupling. The entire team assembled in the control room as the experiment was set up. Work was going on furiously, but the atmosphere was light, the team working together easily, finalizing the settings that would put the huge apparatus into drive.

"I was trying to break up the standing wave," Eddie explained to Professor Bucholtz. "First I thought it was too rough, so I smoothed out the inner surface. And then I thought that maybe it was too smooth, so I sandblasted it a little, then, I don't know . . ." Eddie shrugged. "Somehow, in the middle of the night I started to get a consistent six-micron dispersion size of the droplets. So I didn't touch a thing and I brought it in here.

Lily Sinclair looked disapproving. "Are you telling me it was just a fluke? That you couldn't duplicate it?"

"Well . . ." said Eddie. "I could try."

"And you didn't computer model it at all?" she asked sharply. "So if you walk out of here tonight and get hit by a bus while you're riding that motorcycle of yours, then that's it. We have no way of duplicating the work you've done."

"I'll just have to ride that motorcycle of mine real careful." Eddie grinned, refusing to let her bring him down from his triumph. "Sorry, Lily. Sometimes, in the real world you just got to whack on stuff till it works or breaks. There I was trapped in reality. Again."

Lu Chen looked up from his desk and grinned at Eddie, he alone recognizing the quote.

"Never to return to his home planet or dimension . . ." Chen said, as if completing half of a password.

"What are you two babbling about?" Lily asked, frowning.

"Spawn," said Chen. "Mutant guy."

She looked at Eddie. "You're a mutant guy?"

"Maybe," said Eddie.

"Well, that might explain a few things . . ."

The professor had been checking gauges and stats as they zipped across the screen on the computer bank. Suddenly, he clapped his hands. "Okay, boys and girls. It's time. Start my bath, please."

Lily made a final adjustment on her control panel, then Lu Chen started throwing big switches. As the power went on-line, the air in the room seemed to tremble and vibrate, though if it was from the sudden surge of energy through the device or merely the tension of the experimenters, it was hard to tell.

"Main power," Chen announced.

The giant Lucite tank of superpurified water began to fill quickly, the liquid streaming into the receptacle.

Another technician hit a bank of switches, and a bank of capacitors began to charge, a low hum filling the room. All eyes were on the reaction tank, gas hissing into it as the pressure became unequal between the two tanks. Now water was being transferred into the reaction tank, hitting the hot distillation coil and beginning to steam, the vapor raising the temperature in the laboratory.

"Reaction regulator, please," said Professor Bucholtz, his voice low and controlled.

Eddie was watching the experiment intently, his eyes locked on the LEDs as data strobed across the screens.

"Signal piezoelectric transducers," said Bucholtz.

"Yes, sir," Chen said and activated the next set of signals. Computer screens burst into life, monitoring the images and waveforms in the reaction chamber and the reaction regulator.

The bubbles in the reaction chamber boiled frantically, then coalesced into a single large bubble several inches in diameter, swirling through the tank. As Chen pushed up the power the bubble began to glow.

"Sonoluminescence," Chen muttered.

"The spectrometer is at a hundred thousand degrees Kelvin," Lily intoned. The tension in the room was palpable now. The power, the heat, and the stress points of the apparatus itself made the experiment unstable and possibly dangerous if something should go wrong. The next phase of the experiment was the most hazardous, and everyone in the room knew it.

"Lasers, please," said the professor. It seemed that the riskier the phase of the experiment, the quieter his voice became.

Chen fired the lasers, two sharp blue beams hitting and bisecting the bubble. The insistent hum from the capacitors increased in intensity, arcing toward a loud, high-pitched whining.

All the temperature indicators raced upward, blasting through 1 million degrees in a split second, then 2 million, then 3, then 5 million degrees Kelvin. When the temperature tipped 6 million, the capacitors triggered automatically, sending a power surge to the lasers.

The bubble in the tank grew brighter, shimmering in a harsh blue-white light. The entire laboratory was lit by the glow, the brightness, like magnesium fire, making the shadows darker.

"Twenty million degrees Kelvin," Lily Sinclair declared.

Oxygen and hydrogen were being driven off and sent to the collection tanks. Spare gasses were ignited and burned off every few seconds or so, brilliant orange flame flashing in the blast furnace.

Then, suddenly, the computer screens froze, filled with garbled data. A warning klaxon sounded.

"It's going critical," uttered Lily. She shot a nervous glance at the professor. But he sat still, calmly watching the apparatus he had designed start to shake, the electrical connections sparking and shorting out. The pressure in the mechanism grew too high for the seals to hold and they started bursting, each explosion as loud as a rifle shot. Eddie winced as they blew out.

Bucholtz sighed. "Okay, shut it down. Shut it down. The whole thing is too unstable."

Lu Chen hit the circuit breakers and cut the power. The orange flame in the blast furnace died, and the lab was plunged into a profound and rather depressed silence. Lily closed her laptop computer with a loud snap.

Every member of the team looked at the broken machinery, wondering if they had made the crucial mistake that had ruined the experiment—every member, that is, except Professor Bucholtz.

"Oh, for God's sake," the professor said, laughing loudly. "Don't be so damn gloomy."

CHAPTER THREE

All the scientists gathered in Professor Bucholtz's office, most of them poring over the blueprints hunting for the smallest mistake, the tiniest glitch that might have brought down the experiment. Lily Sinclair's fingers were flying over the keys of her laptop computer as she checked and rechecked every figure and equation that had gone into the calibrations.

Eddie Kasalivich was on the far side of the lab, studiously avoiding the white-coat crowd. He was hunched over his workbench, using a dental mirror to examine the inside of the nozzle he had made. The men and women in Bucholtz's office were scientists, each of them armed with at least two advanced degrees, doctorates and masters degrees in physics, chemistry, mathematics . . . Eddie had never finished college. He was a technician, a hands-on machinist—and a damn good one. But in the pecking order of academia he was as far down the chain of command as you could get. Most of the scientists assumed that the techies were lower forms of life who were only there to do the bidding of the people with brains.

The two scientists who did not feel this way were Lu Chen and Professor Bucholtz himself.

The professor looked at his glum team and shook his head, laughing to himself. "You know, you're all too damn worried for my taste."

The scientists looked up from the blueprints, Lily's fingers paused above the keyboard. Even Eddie turned around and faced Bucholtz.

"You think Alexander Fleming knew that the right spore was going to fly through the window, land on a petrie dish, and give the world penicillin?" He looked from face to face, like a teacher who thinks he has a class of promising students but discovers to his chagrin that they are just a collection of dullards. The professor sighed heavily.

"Well, of course he didn't," Bucholtz continued. "Sometimes science is just about having your mind open. Open it up, don't think about it—just let the answer fall in. It's as simple as that."

As he spoke, James Shannon quietly stole into the room, hanging back a little, rolling a sweet Cuban cigar—a Montecristo Number 4—between his well-manicured fingers. He smiled. He always enjoyed Professor Bucky Bucholtz's impromptu little homilies.

Like Eddie, Shannon stood apart from the rest of the team. He was rich and they were not. His hair was perfectly cut, his clothes faultless, his shoes hand-made in London. In contrast to the usual uniform of the scientists, the clothes they wore under those white coats—old jeans, beat-up running shoes—James Shannon stood out like a dandy in a refugee camp.

The professor was warming to his subject. "Most people don't have their minds open," he said. "They've trained themselves to think in one way and one way only. That is not good. But don't worry. The answer to our little set of problems is there. We'll find it. But first we need to open our minds. It sounds easy, but that might be the most difficult lesson we learn from this experiment." Bucky Bucholtz caught sight of James Shannon and smiled.

"Are you getting worried, Mr. Shannon?" Bucholtz asked. "Worried about throwing good money after bad?"

"Bad money, Professor?" said Shannon. "There's not a penny spent so far that I consider wasted."

"But your foundation has spent a fortune on us," Professor Bucholtz protested. "The least we can do is give you some cause for worry."

Shannon laughed. "That's very thoughtful of you," he said. "Thanks. I'll see if I can find some time in my schedule for worrying."

The team thought Professor Bucholtz knew everything, but Shannon had long ago identified a wide gap in the professor's field of knowledge. Bucholtz did not know a damn thing about money. He could not understand that the paltry millions the foundation had put into the coffers of the Bessemer Project were only a fraction of the money earmarked for this undertaking. Furthermore, should the foundation end up spending 10, 20, 50 million dollars on Professor Bucholtz and his experiments, the returns would be immense if the project proved to be a success.

And they would not necessarily be returns measured in financial terms.

If Professor Bucholtz and his scientists could draw clean energy from hydrogen, then the foundation would benefit in money, of course, but also in something more precious—in power, clout on a national and global scale. And that was worth as much money as it took to achieve.

Bucholtz appeared to have already lost interest in the question. He turned his attention back to the team.

"We learned something very important today," he said. "We found another way that did not work. Do you know how many substances Edison tested before he found the correct material for the filament in a lightbulb? Something like nine hundred. He tried bamboo and human hair . . . But one day he found tungsten, the incandescent bulb was born, and the world lit up."

The professor slid his glasses up onto his forehead as if raising the visor of an invisible helmet. He rubbed his eyes vigorously, as if trying to massage his brain behind his eye sockets.

"I am going home," he said. "I'm going to feed the cat and then go to sleep. Maybe the answer will come to me in a dream. I would suggest that you all get busy . . ." Professor Bucholtz made for the door. ". . . doing something not associated, in any way whatsoever, with this experiment . . ."

As the door closed behind him, the members of the team stirred. A Czech physicist named Screbenski fired up the mainframe computer and began running not data from the experiment, but the most powerful application of the computer game Myst in the western hemisphere.

"How can you waste your time on that?" Lily Sinclair asked sourly. "There are so many more interesting things to do."

"To you, perhaps," said Screbenski in his heavily accented English. "The things that make you happy make you wise. Have you never heard that, Lily?"

"No," said Sinclair. "Who said it?"

Screbenski looked puzzled. "I did."

Lu Chen took the professor's advice as well. He dug a copy of *Spawn* out of the thicket of papers on his desk, propped his feet on his computer console, and started to read, his lips forming the words carefully.

Shannon looked at the Czech playing a computer game and the young Chinese scientist reading a garish comic book. He walked over to Eddie and tapped him on the shoulder.

"You," he said, feigning a mock severity. "I want a word with you."

Eddie was the only member of the team who had not followed the professor's advice. He was still fiddling with his nozzle, puzzling over it, trying to figure out what went wrong.

"Hey, whatever it is, don't blame me," said Eddie. "I was someplace else at the time."

Despite the differences of age and income, there was an easy relationship between Shannon and Eddie. They were the only two outsiders in the experiment, the only two excluded by science.

"Are you the one responsible for the sudden outbreak of American popular culture in this lab? We've got a Czech playing computer games and a Chinese man reading comic books. That brain of Chen's is a delicate instrument, and as I recall, comic books have all the delicacy of a ball-peen hammer."

Eddie smiled. "Then that just shows you haven't read a comic book in a long, long time."

"You're surprised by that?"

"No. I'm helping Chen understand more about life here in the U.S. of A. Spawn, the son of the devil, is basically good, but sometimes that old genetic makeup breaks through. Can't avoid the id, you know."

"Spawn?" said Shannon unimpressed. "I'm impressed."

"But I think Mutant Guy is the answer for Chen," Eddie continued.

"Mutant Guy?" said Shannon in the same deadpan tone of voice. "I can't wait to hear about him."

"Well," said Eddie. "He's kind of like Howard the Duck, but not at all. If you see what I mean."

"Clear as day."

"I mean, he's a scientist from another planet, not some stupid talking duck," said Eddie, his voice full of enthusiasm. "But he is trapped in a world he never made. Which is a pain in the ass."

"Sort of like you and me," said Shannon.

Eddie nodded. "Exactly."

CHAPTER FOUR

Eddie knew that he should do exactly what Professor Bucholtz suggested. Forget the Bessemer Project for a couple of hours, go to a movie, watch TV, read a book . . . even hit a bar, have a couple of beers, play some pool. Have some fun. The trouble was, to Eddie fun *was* working on the mechanical bits and pieces of the vast, complex apparatus.

He left the lab, mounted his motorcycle, and blasted across town to the loft he kept on the other side of Chicago. It was his lair, a large open space crammed with equipment and both power and hand tools. A small portion of the space was given over to Eddie's meager living needs—a galley kitchen, a mattress on the floor, an armchair, and a battered TV set.

He sat at his workbench until the small hours of the morning, carefully recrafting his own home version of the piece of the apparatus known as the reaction regulator. This he hooked up to a tabletop version of the sonoluminescence device. Eddie had rewired his entire loft—in contravention of a half a dozen Chicago building codes—to allow enough power to run smaller versions of the experiment at home.

When the direct current hit his model, the small glowing bubble in the chamber of the device came in about the size of a BB, the light it emitted unsteady and isochronal. He tried to stabilize the minute orb, but the little dot bobbed and wobbled unsteadily, refusing to steady out.

Eddie cursed under his breath and stared at the dancing ball as if it would talk back to him and explain the problem. Then someone pounded on his door. He glanced at the clock on the workbench—12:45 A.M. Eddie knew that his visitor could only be one person.

Anton, Eddie's next-door neighbor, seemed to have no steady job and certainly kept erratic hours. It wasn't out of the ordinary for him to knock on the door of the loft at two, even three in the morning, dropping in just to chat or, in this case, to ask a favor of Eddie.

"Oh good," said Anton, wandering into the loft. "You're home." He held up a greasy shaft of metal. "You said you'd fix my tie rod . . ."

Anton was a gearhead like Eddie, but he lacked Eddie's skill and was not nearly as well equipped. Spread out in Anton's apartment were the thousand parts of an old Harley-Davidson Knuckle Head twin cylinder that Anton said he was "restoring." Though over the years Eddie had put just as much effort into the reconstruction of the old bike as its owner had.

It was plain that Eddie was not much in the mood to work on a piece of the Harley right then, but if he didn't do it now he'd have to do it some other time. Anton could be very persistent.

"Let me have a look at it," said Eddie. He took the shaft of metal from Anton and peered at it under the light. "The threads are stripped."

"Yeah, that's what I figured," said Anton, shrugging. "But I don't have one of them, you know, rethreading things."

"Tapping collar," said Eddie.

"Yeah," said Anton. "One of them."

Eddie clamped the tie rod into the cutting bed

of the machine and started it up, lowering the milling edge onto the steel shaft. He hadn't bothered to lubricate the tie rod, so when the teeth hit the steel there was a terrible scream. As the scream increased in pitch and volume, Eddie noticed that the bubble in the tank started to flare, growing more intense and bright, then stabilized.

Eddie lifted the milling edge and the glow diminished, the BB dancing and tottering once more. He cranked down on the tie rod again, cutting more threads, the scream driving the power up in the reaction regulator. Eddie couldn't take his eyes off the device. He lowered the mill again.

"Hey," Anton protested. "I don't need threads all the way down the neck, you know. You're gonna fuck it up."

"Shut up," said Eddie. He reached to a bank of instruments, turned on an oscilloscope, setting it to record and lock, then cut another set of spiral threads into the tie rod. As the scream hit the scope there was an instantaneous trace on the screen of the cathode ray tube, recording the oscillations of the voltage and current.

The tie rod was now threaded from one end

to the other. "Here you go," said Eddie, handing the warm shaft back to Anton.

"Thanks," said Anton, looking rather dubious.

Eddie hardly paid attention. The tie rod may have been ruined, but he had the feeling that the Bessemer Project was back on track.

When the old black rotary phone next to Professor Bucholtz's bed rang at three that morning, the old man hardly stirred. By the time the eighteenth or nineteenth ring echoed through his silent house, Bucholtz's eyes began to flutter—then, suddenly, he sat bolt upright in bed and began fumbling for the phone and his glasses.

"Hmmmm," he said into the receiver.

"We were totally right. At the same time we were totally wrong," said Eddie. He was pacing the living space of the loft, pulling the snarled telephone cord to the limit of its twenty feet.

Bucholtz blinked behind his glasses. "Who's that? Eddie? My God, what time is it?"

"Who cares?" said Eddie. "It was the reaction regulator. I had milled it wrong. I pushed it to the resonance peak."

Professor Bucholtz was wide awake now. He understood exactly what his machinist was talking about. He snapped on the light.

"You did what I told you to do," said Bucholtz. "The trouble is you did it too well."

"Well, that's not how I'd put it," said Eddie.

"Never mind what you'd call it," said Bucholtz impatiently. "Tell me if the thing is stable."

Eddie peered at the regulator. The oscilloscope was locked on the same wave going to the regulator and the piezoelectric.

"Totally," said Eddie.

"My God," Bucholtz gasped.

Eddie peered into the reaction regulator, the point of light glowing steady and bright like a small star.

CHAPTER FIVE

This time it worked.

Bucholtz led his team into the lab the next morning, and with renewed industry they went about setting up for the experiment once again. It took the better part of the day to get the procedure up and running again. Night was falling when the experiment went on-line once more.

Lily was locked on the bank of computers, her eyes flicking from screen to screen as data poured out in various forms, graphics, and figures. Chen was swallowing hard, his mouth dry.

The lasers had passed through the stage of sonoluminescence and had been shut down. As soon as the light show ended the bubble stayed in place, glowing a steady blue-white.

Bucholtz chortled in delight. The flame grew, and the room glowed. Chen finally found his voice.

"We have total sonoluminescence," Chen stammered. "It's . . . it's self-sustaining. Completely."

The meters were pinned at the highest readings, straining to go higher, but there was no room behind the glass.

"We're off the levels," said Lily. "The power has topped out at maximum apex." She glanced at the readings. "And them some."

Bucholtz quickly wiped away a tear. "We've done it," he said softly. "We've finally done it . . ."

For a long moment no one could speak, the only sound in the lab being the bleating of the computers, the dull boom of the burn-off in the blast chamber, and the chattering of the printers as paper poured out black with figures. No one moved, every person in the room stood rooted to the spot, staring as the apparatus went through the cycle perfectly, feeding water into the chamber, separating it into component parts, storing the energy, and igniting the burn-off. It looked as if could go on forever.

Finally it was James Shannon who broke the silence. "You know," he said. "I think I had better go by some champagne . . ."

Shannon returned with a dozen bottles of champagne, a couple of really good bottles for a round of toasts, the rest mediocre no-name stuff. He knew that the function of champagne on occasions like this was the same as champagne drunk in the locker rooms of winning ball clubs. You squirted it, glugged it, dumped it on the heads of your team members . . . It was a symbol of victory. Besides, Shannon wondered, what kind of wine would really complement the half-dozen large-with-everything-on-them pizzas that had been ordered in?

Someone found a radio and turned it up loud, the party cranking up a notch, and the sheer euphoria of the moment being intensified by the liberal doses of champagne Shannon dispensed.

Even Lily Sinclair lightened up, wandering around the lab, laughing and joking with every person there—even Eddie—while gulping from a plastic cup of champagne. She did not know how many times it had been refilled and did not care. She did not completely let go, of course; she remembered that this was a moment that had to be captured and recorded for history. She dug a small point-and-shoot camera out of her desk and started to try to round up all the merry-making scientists.

"Everybody!" she called. "Come on now, we gotta take the picture. In the years to come a lot of people are going to claim they were here at this moment. This is gonna be your proof."

It wasn't easy to get everyone formed up. Academicians don't get the chance to drink a lot of champagne of any quality, and they were all a little tipsy. Finally, they formed two ragged ranks in front of the apparatus, leaving a space next to Professor Bucholtz for Lily.

She rested the camera on the edge of Eddie's workbench and tried to key the timer. But Shannon stopped her.

"I'll take the picture," he said, picking up the camera. "C'mon, get in your place."

"Oh, come on," Lily protested. "You should be in it too, Mr. Shannon." She took another gulp of champagne. "After all, it was your money that paid for all this. There wouldn't have been an experiment if it hadn't been for you."

Shannon laughed good-naturedly. "Don't worry about that. Bucky would have found the money someplace." Lily couldn't have known, of course, that the last time James Shannon had had his picture taken was the day he graduated from college. He had no intention of having his picture taken again. Ever.

She didn't argue, but took her place next to Professor Bucholtz, a huge smile on her face.

"Okay," Shannon ordered. "Everybody say—"

"Cheese," said Chen.

"No," said Shannon, laughing. "I want all of you to say, 'Oh my God, we really did it!'"

They all tried to say it in unison, but it came out a ragged mess. "Oh my God! We really did it . . ."

Shannon fired off six or eight shots, continuing to photograph as Bucholtz stepped forward, his plastic cup raised.

"This is to all of you," he said. "To all of your hard work and dedication over the many years."

They all sipped. Then Bucholtz spoke again. "And especially to Eddie," the professor said solemnly. "The man who found the last little piece of the puzzle. Thank you."

Eddie felt his face flush, disconcerted at being singled out for special recognition. He tried to say something self-deprecating, but his voice caught in his throat, so he contented himself with raising his glass and doing a little sort of bob with his head in Bucholtz's direction.

He was engulfed with self-consciousness, so he failed at that moment to notice that Lily Sinclair was watching him with a new-found curiosity.

The party went on, the scientists and the technicians letting the barriers down for once. Chen and Eddie, of course, without such inhibitions to start out with, had adapted science to their celebration. They had managed to rig up small hydrogen balloons, steel nuts dangling from the bottom as counterweights, the balloons floating over the heat of a Bunsen burner and bursting into flame. Each time one ignited the two men giggled like idiots.

In a quiet corner of the lab, Bucholtz and Shannon stood together, heads close, talking softly but intensely.

"You have every reason to be proud," said Shannon. "It's a breakthrough of unprecedented import."

"I understand that," Bucholtz replied. "That's why it's so important that we move quickly to—"

Shannon held his hand up, palm out like a policeman stopping a line of traffic, cutting off the professor.

"You're going to have to trust me on this one, Bucky," Shannon said shortly. "Please understand me. Caution is the watchword. We've stuck with you every step of the way. Now you're going to have to step back. Please."

Bucholtz took a deep breath and nodded. "Okay, okay, James. I understand completely." But as he turned away there was a look on his face that suggested he had other plans in mind . . .

CHAPTER SIX

The day Lu Chen received his first paycheck in U.S. dollars, he took the whole thing and went out and paid every penny as a down payment on a brand-new Camaro. It was far too powerful a machine for anyone whose experience of automobiles had been restricted to underpowered tin cans produced by the People's Republic of China. There was a running joke around the lab that the combination of Chen and Camaro added up to too much car controlled by not enough driver. Professor Bucholtz had declared that he would never ride in the jet-black muscle car.

"One of the first things I learned in physics

was that force equals mass times acceleration. Chen, it's nothing personal, but I don't feel good with you putting out that much force with that much mass and acceleration. Sorry."

But tonight, things were different. As the party broke up, Chen got behind the wheel of his powerful car and revved the big engine. Thrusting his head out the window he called out to Professor Bucholtz.

"Come on, Professor, let me give you a ride . . ."

Bucholtz laughed. "Okay, Chen." He pulled open the passenger door. "Tonight I'm feeling very lucky."

The Camaro roared off into the night, Eddie shaking his head as Chen crunched the gear into second. As the sound of the big engine died away, Eddie heard another grinding, this one from the starter of Lily Sinclair's Toyota Camry. Eddie walked over and rapped on the driver's side window.

Lily jumped, startled, then opened the door and got out, pointing at the car accusingly. Eddie noticed that she was a little unsteady on her feet, the champagne having gone to her head.

"It won't start," she said.

Eddie looked in, glanced at the dashboard,

then turned the key, turning off the electrical system in the car.

"I'm not surprised," he said. "It's out of gas."

"Well, thank you, Mr. Technical Wizard Mutant Guy," she said with a slightly crooked smile. "But no gas? That hardly seems fair . . . when all we do around here is deal with gasses."

"It's a different kind of gas," said Eddie.

"I know that," Lily insisted with the forthrightness and certainty of the slightly tipsy. "But there should be gas. I need to go somewhere."

Eddie started to lead Lily toward his motorcycle. "You shouldn't drive, anyhow. Let me take you home." Then he stopped. The night was cold and there was an icy wind blowing off Lake Michigan. Contrary to popular belief, alcohol was not antifreeze. Indeed, Lily was already chilled to the bone. He could feel her slim body shivering against his.

"You'll freeze to death."

"I think I already have," she said, her teeth chattering.

"Where do you live?"

"Kimball and Fifty-fourth," she said.

"Okay." He started to walk her away from the laboratory building, and she was just drunk enough to allow herself to be led along, docile, it not occurring to her to ask where she was going or why.

The answer was pretty prosaic. Eddie marched her to a bus stop and the two of them stood there in a pool of light cast by a streetlight. There was enough alcohol in her bloodstream to make the usually standoffish Lily Sinclair slightly flirtatious and, for her, impulsive.

"How come I don't know you better?" she said, swaying slightly. "Are you shy? Or is it just that I'm a snob?"

"You're a snob," said Eddie. He spoke gently, without venom.

"I'll bet you're smart, though." She stared at him as if his IQ might have been tattooed on his forehead. "Bucky and Shannon wouldn't have hired you if you weren't smart."

Eddie smiled. "Maybe they made a mistake. Even the most brilliant people make a mistake once in a while."

"Do you?"

"I didn't say I was brilliant."

Lily shrugged. "Well, even if you're not, I hope you're proud. Really proud of being a part of this."

Eddie was proud—more than she could know.

"It takes everyone working together to do a

thing like this, you know," she said with the vehemence of a drunk. "Just being on the team is a . . ." She paused, trying to find the perfect word, then gave up. "It's a great thing, don't you think? Even if you're not one of the—" She stopped, aware even in a drink-fogged state she was about to commit a faux pas.

"Not one of the what?" asked Eddie innocently.

"You know what I mean."

Eddie laughed. "Yup. I know exactly what you mean." He looked up the street. "Here comes the bus."

There were a few sleepy men and women on the battered old city bus. Second-shift workers making their way home after a long night on the job or those who had just woken up and who were headed to the employment that kept them busy till dawn.

The lights inside the bus seemed to subdue Lily slightly, and in that moment of clarity the enormity of what had happened that night began to come down on her. She was silent for a few blocks, then she turned to Eddie.

"We've changed the world," she said soberly, though she could still feel the wine. "It will never be the same after what happened tonight.

Do you realize that? None of these people know it . . ."

Lily gestured toward the listless passengers and the people who were asleep in the houses they passed. "No one knows it. But the world has changed forever. They'll wake up in the morning, and everything will seem the same as it was yesterday. But it won't be. They don't know that yet, but starting tonight the world is a different place than it was this morning. And we were there."

Eddie opened his mouth to say something goofy and fun, but it struck him that everything she said was true. The weight of the event pressed on him, and he found himself wanting to tell her something, how it made him feel, deep down . . .

He breathed deep. "Let me tell you something. It's important." Glancing over at Lily, he found that his words might have been important to him but not, unfortunately, to Lily. She was sound asleep, her soft cheek pressed against his left shoulder.

It took thirty-five minutes for the bus to run its course, yet Lily did not wake until Eddie pressed the signal for a stop.

"We're at Fifty-fourth," he called to her as he gently shook her by the shoulder. "Hey, wake up. This is our stop."

"Huh?" Lily sat up, blinking in the light, unable to remember where she was for a moment. The hair on one side of her head was plastered down.

Eddie led her by the hand and guided her down the steps of the bus. "You're home," he said.

He looked up at the house. "Oh no," he said. "No you're not. This is Bucholtz's house." It had become a tradition over the years to celebrate team birthdays and major holidays at Bucholtz's house, so Eddie knew it well. He had never seen any part of the house besides the front living room on the ground floor; he wondered if he was going to tonight.

"You didn't know?" said Lily as she fussed with her hair. "I live here."

"I didn't know," he said.

"Don't look so shocked," she said giggling. "There's nothing, you know, between Professor Bucholtz and me. Except that I'm his star student, and he's the most brilliant man who ever lived."

She started up the steep stone stairs of the

stoop, tripping almost immediately. "Oooops," she said.

"Do you need help?"

Lily nodded emphatically. "You know," she said, digging in her purse for her house keys, "I think I do." She handed over the keys. "I'm all the way to the top. Third floor."

Eddie gazed up at the windows. No light showed. He wondered if Chen had delivered the professor home yet—and what he might think if he found his "star student" and his technician on the stairs of his house in the small hours of the morning. Knowing Bucky, he'd laugh.

Climbing the three flights of stairs with a tipsy, exhausted girl in tow was not easy. By the time they got to the top floor, Eddie could not tell which was the more powerful influence on her, alcohol or fatigue.

She stopped on the third floor landing and grinned crookedly at him. "Is this what drunk is?" she asked.

"You never been drunk before?" Eddie asked.

"I've never been this before . . ." She led the way, stumbling, toward the door to her room.

Lily's bedroom was high up under the eaves of the old Victorian house, large, with a fireplace and a bay window. She dropped onto the bed and slipped off her shoes, sinking with a sigh into the pile of pillows.

"Lily's too serious," she mumbled. "Lily's way, way too serious. That's her problem . . ."

Eddie looked at the six diplomas hanging on the wall, the names of some of them jumping out at him: MIT, CalTech, Institute for Advanced Study—along with the Latin phrases: magna cum laude, summa cum laude . . .

"Who says that?" he asked. "Who says you're no fun?"

Lily's eyes were closed. "Everybody says it," Lily said dreamily. "Everybody says Lily's no fun . . ."

And then she was asleep, her arms curled around her pillow, as if holding on to it for comfort. Eddie tucked a blanket around her, noticing that, as she slipped deeper into sleep, the hard-edged scientist with the slew of degrees vanished, replaced with the soft planes and gentle curves of a very beautiful woman . . .

A bus rumbled by under the window. That, Eddie thought, would be the last of the night. And it meant that Eddie was faced with a long, cold walk back to the laboratory and his motorcycle.

CHAPTER SEVEN

Chen was driving erratically and too fast down Highland Boulevard, heading for a country-western bar he knew when Professor Bucholtz let out a little yelp and slapped his forehead.

"Chen!" he shouted. "Stop the car!"

Chen hit the brakes hard, and the car slithered to a halt. Only because it was so late and there was no traffic on the road did the sleek Camaro not end up with a trunkful of a car from behind.

"I'm sorry, Bucky," said Chen contritely. "I'll drive a little slower." He put the car in gear again, and the vehicle lurched forward a few feet.

"No, no, no," the professor said quickly. "That's not it. We have to go back to the lab immediately."

"Did you forget something?"

"No," said Bucholtz. "It's not that . . ." He could feel Chen's questioning eyes on his face. "It's just that I would feel better if I had all the data on the experiment at home with me. I want to take it home and review it."

Chen looked surprised. "*All* of it?" The young scientist thought of the volumes of data, the thousands of computer disks that comprised the full extent of the work done on the Bessemer Project.

"No," said Professor Bucholtz. "Just the data on the successful procedure. The one we ran tonight."

"Okay," said Chen dubiously. He pushed the big car through a clumsy three-point turn then headed back the way they had just come.

The professor was silent on the trip back to the lab. In spite of the euphoria of the successful test run earlier that evening Bucholtz was worried about his conversation with Shannon. If it were up to the professor he would gather all the Bessemer information together and disseminate it via the Internet to anyone who cared to download and decipher it. He knew of thousands of scientists the world over who would be able to render it in terms that laymen could understand. From there, Bessemer-type refiners could be constructed—the global revolution could begin almost at once.

But Shannon had told him that the foundation needed to develop a strategy for the distribution of the data, that they had to proceed cautiously and make sure that, in his words, "this revolutionary discovery did not fall into the wrong hands." As far as Bucholtz was concerned there were no "wrong hands." He had pretended to agree with Shannon, intending to send out the information first thing in the morning. However, now, in the dead of the night, he had the uneasy feeling that he didn't have the luxury of waiting the few hours until dawn.

It struck the professor that he didn't really know much about the foundation Shannon represented. In the excitement of getting funds for his experiments, it had not occurred to Bucholtz to ask where the money was coming from in the first place. All he really knew was that the foundation had been a generous—extremely generous—supporter of his research.

Professor Bucholtz had benefited from foundation grants before. In his experience he was forever filling out forms and glad-handing officials to get the needed resources. Strict accounting of almost every penny spent was the norm. Shannon's employers, however, had merely opened their coffers, and the money had gushed out in a steady torrent.

The more he thought about it, the more apprehensive he became. He decided he had been a fool.

"Chen," said the Professor. "You can go a little faster."

"You got her," answered Chen with a grin, stomping hard on the gas pedal, pushing it to the floor.

They reached the laboratory in a matter of minutes, but instead of parking in the main lot, Professor Bucholtz had Chen drive by, then pull around to the rear exit. There had been no vehicle in the parking lot other than Lily's car and Eddie's big old motorcycle. No threat there.

"This seems very silly," said Chen with a little giggle. "It is much easier to go in the front."

Bucholtz nodded as he unlocked the rusty, rarely used rear door. "I know that," he said, nodding vigorously. It was far too hard to explain to this boy that he was worried about security. Better to make a joke. "But I must beg you to indulge the whims and quirks of an elderly madman."

"No problem," said Chen, pleased with himself for remembering to use this Americanism.

They stepped into the lab and flicked on some of the lights. "Chen, you get on the computer and make copies of everything on the experiment, then put a computer security lock on them. But I want all the specs, all the test results from tonight, the whole procedure from start to finish. Understand?"

Chen nodded. "I do, Professor Bucky, but we don't have spec on one piece. Nothing on the nozzle."

Bucholtz shrugged. "Well, that's Eddie for you. He does it all by hand then works backwards on the specs. Pull the nozzle off the device and get the calipers on it. Be as precise as you can, but don't take too much time.

"You got her again," said Chen, heading into the shadows, making for the computer control.

Then, from somewhere deep in the cavernous lab came a sound, a clatter as a heap of specification manuals were knocked from a desk.

"Is someone still here?" Bucholtz asked.

Chen giggled again. "I think we have rats in here, Professor. Nothing to worry about."

Neither of them heard the small, unmarked van glide into the front parking lot and come to a halt.

Chen set up the computers and started to copy all of the information from the hard drives onto a series of floppy disks. A few hours of running the Bessemer apparatus generated tens of millions of bits of data; even using the high-speed computers the lab was equipped with, the transfer of information was going to take a couple of hours or more. That was fine with Chen—it was going to take some time for him to record the specs on the nozzle, having to do all the work by hand.

He lugged a tool chest out of one of the storerooms and laid out a set of calipers and micrometers on Eddie's workbench, then grabbed a wrench and climbed into the guts of the device.

The nozzle was so flawlessly made and fit so perfectly that Chen had no trouble removing it from the body of the machine. He took it back to the bench and settled down with a notebook. It was time-consuming and rather boring work, and Chen's brain was fogged with the effects of the champagne as well as simple fatigue. It was hard going to keep his attention properly focused, so when he heard something scrabbling around in the shadows, Chen welcomed the diversion. He grabbed a rat trap from a corner and with a grin on his face went hunting.

Chen was crawling around on his hands and knees under one of the consoles when, about thirty feet away, he saw what he thought was a pair of heavily shod feet. Not Bucholtz's battered wingtip shoes, but a pair of black workboots. In the split second it took for him to blink and look back, the feet had vanished.

"Professor Bucky?" Chen called out.

There was no answer. Chen felt a cold wave of fear break over him. The trap in his hand snapped closed, and Chen jumped. He smiled nervously to himself, trying to tell himself that there was nothing wrong.

But then he heard footsteps again and once again he froze. "Chen?" shouted Bucholtz. "You called me?"

Lu Chen felt a huge swell of relief rise in him. "No, no, Professor Bucky. It's nothing."

Bucholtz, sitting at his desk, heard his assistant's voice, shrugged, and went back to the pile of papers spread out in front of him.

Silently, the door of the office swung open, and Bucholtz sensed rather than heard or saw the two men who stole into the room. Both men were dressed in dark clothes and ski masks. Both men carried large-caliber handguns.

"Who are you?" Professor Bucholtz demanded, jumping to his feet. "What do you want?"

"I want you to sit down," said one of the men calmly. "I want to have a little talk with you."

Bucholtz did not move, but stared defiantly at the thugs. He was not going to sit. He was not going to talk. And he knew where this evening would end. Never had he imagined that the happiest day of his life would also be his last.

CHAPTER EIGHT

Eddie was chilled through and worn out by the time he made it back to the lab and was grateful when he finally swung a leg over his bike and turned the key. Before firing up the engine, though, he noticed the van parked square in front of the entrance of the laboratory and a sliver of light showing under the big steel double doors. He did not recognize the small truck, no one on the team drove one, and the commercial cleaners only came during the day when Bucholtz could keep an eye on them. Eddie shrugged and was about to get going when he realized that he could hear something, the hum and whine of the experiment going on-line.

Hopping off his bike, Eddie moved stealthily toward the front entrance, his heart starting to pound fast when he saw that the door was ajar and the heavy-duty lock had been yanked out of its housing. He pushed into the lab, stopping in the dimly lit corridor, a room usually so familiar now looking foreign and strange. From the interior of the facility came the sound of hissing and thrashing, noises he had never heard before, not in connection with any experiment run in the lab during the time of his tenure. He advanced another step into the room.

"Anybody home?" he called, but his voice was snuffed out by the noise coming from within. He glanced into Bucholtz's office. It was lit only by the green glow of his computer screen, but Eddie could see that someone was sitting in the high-backed leather chair behind the desk.

"Bucky?" Eddie stepped into the doorway. "Bucky, you okay?" He snapped on the light. What he saw struck him like a hard blow to the chest, taking his breath away. Professor Bucholtz was slumped in his chair, his face a chalky blue-white, a clear plastic bag knotted around his neck and plastered to his skin with the last inhalation of breath.

"Jesus God!" Eddie dove across the room,

yanked the plastic bag from the professor's head, and pulling him from the chair, laid him flat on the floor. "Oh Jesus, Bucky!"

He opened Bucholtz's mouth and pressed his own mouth against it, trying desperately to breath some life back into the professor's body. Eddie turned his head, breathed deep and then tried again, but the professor did not stir. "Oh, Bucky, come on. Come on!"

Eddie pressed his hands to Bucholtz's chest and pumped frantically, trying to remember the CPR he had been taught years ago.

"Shit, shit, shit." Professor Bucholtz did not respond. Eddie grabbed the phone, but it was dead, the cord having been ripped from the wall. He dashed out of the office and grabbed the phone on Chen's desk, but that one was useless, the cord severed clean through.

Eddie's mind whirled as he stood there, the dead phone in his hand, trying to make sense of the last few minutes. Then he sniffed deeply and realized that the air in the lab was thick with oxygen. In the rear of the room he could see that the feed hoses to the hydrogen tank had been cut and were flapping as gas streamed out. He rushed to the stop valve, but it spun uselessly in his hand.

Eddie started to back away from the tank, his eyes wide with fright. The slightest spark and the lab would erupt in an explosion that would make the destruction of the *Hindenberg* look like a firecracker. He didn't know who was inside running the experiment, and he didn't care. The instant those lasers kicked in, the hydrogen would ignite, and Eddie did not want to be around to see it. He took off, running for the door.

Outside he filled his lungs with sweet night air and ran for his bike, pushing it like a scooter until he was prepared to gamble with the ignition. He kicked the starter and popped the clutch, a short blue flame shooting from the exhaust. Eddie ducked and winced.

"Holy shit!" But there was no explosion. He jumped onto the saddle and blasted away, the engine of the bike screaming at such rough treatment.

Then the lab blew.

Eddie felt the blast before he heard it, a superhot wind hitting him hard in the back, sweeping over him like the beam of a searchlight. Directly behind that came the waves of fire emanating outward in concentric circles; then came a boom like the wrath of God.

Just the sound blast wave was strong enough to knock Eddie from his bike, sending him flying through the hot air, throwing him into a ditch like a broken doll. The air was full of fire and debris, and the only sound was the roaring of the fire.

The initial orb of flame burned off in a few seconds—seconds which seemed to Eddie to last a year or longer. When he summoned up the courage to look over the edge of the ditch he saw a vast fire burning where the laboratory used to be, smaller explosions erupting within the larger fireball as the flames reached the tanks of flammable material that had been stored on the site.

Car alarms were blaring for miles around, and broken glass was falling from windows like snow. Sirens were screaming and getting closer, and a few seconds later the first fire truck raced by him, followed immediately by a dozen more.

Very slowly, Eddie got to his feet and examined himself. His clothes were smoking and smelled of fire, his hair was singed, and there were burns on his hands in the places where his skin had touched the heated metal of his motorcycle handlebars. He couldn't remember his skin blistering nor did the pain register in his stunned, dazed brain. All he could do was stand at the side of the road and watch the emergency vehicles roar past him, as if watching a parade.

That was what he was doing when an EMS worker found him, bandaged his hands, and asked him if he needed anything.

"Yes," Eddie said, as if waking from a trance. "I need a phone."

James Shannon answered on the first ring, and the sound of his voice seemed to rouse Eddie to activity. Suddenly words were pouring from him in a torrent, his speech so fast it was almost incomprehensible.

"Eddie? Eddie?" said Shannon. "Calm down."

Eddie took a deep breath and tried to slow his hammering heart. "The lab," he gasped. "The lab has exploded. There's been an explosion . . ."

Shannon went to the window of his hotel suite and looked eastward. In the distance the sky was lit by an ominous orange glow.

"Oh Christ," he whispered.

CHAPTER NINE

In the cold, clear light of dawn the extent of the devastation became apparent. The laboratory and any part of the old factory that housed it had vanished; in its place smoldered a giant crater and piles of rubble. Dozens of firefighters worked through the smoking ruins, fighting to tamp down the hot spots where the stubborn fire would flare up and burn for a moment.

In the wake of the emergency vehicles had come the media caravan. All of the local Chicago stations along with the three networks and cable news had sent crews to the scene, and the road on either side of the ruin was lined with television vans, their satellite uplink dishes pushed high into the sky.

Policemen had set up barricades keeping back the reporters and the curious onlookers. Inside the barrier, the cops had corralled the members of the team, all of whom had raced for the site the instant they heard the news. Shannon was there too, protective of the team, running interference, keeping the reporters and television crews away from his people.

There was a news lockdown for the time being, so the crews and correspondents had nothing to do but stand in front of the smoking pit and speculate for the viewer at home.

Eddie got close enough to one to listen.

". . . although according to sources at the university level, the mill had been converted into a site for the experimental production of hydrogen fuel, it was not supposed to be dangerous."

The reporter looked sternly into the lens of the camera, then added:

"But tell that to this once-peaceful neighborhood whose quiet was shattered last night."

Eddie shook his head. This wasn't a neighborhood, it was an industrial zone, but the reporter made it sound like they had been making poison gas on a Norman Rockwell Main Street.

As he listened, two nondescript government-issue sedans pulled up to the scene, and before the doors even opened one of the cops manning the barricades nudged another in the ribs.

"Uh-oh," he said. "Feds."

Two agents got out of the first car, the first, a tall, grizzled FBI lifer wearing the standard-issue gray sack suit; the second, his assistant, a smaller man, but dressed almost identically. It was easy to peg them as Feds—they had that clean-cut, flag-pin-in-the-lapel look that somehow suggested a Catholic high–schooling in the depths of the 1950s. They were men who had joined the bureau when J. Edgar Hoover still ruled the FBI and set the standards.

From the second car came the rest of the team. Three men, two women, all of them wearing the FBI uniform but younger than the other two—and of a racial mix that Mr. Hoover would not have countenanced. Women agents were bad enough, but in this team one of the women was Hispanic, as was one of the men; another man was Asian, another black. The remaining woman was Jewish, and J. Edgar had always maintained a low opinion of members of that faith. He didn't think they could be considered "real" Americans.

The two lead men, Agents Ford and Doyle, looked over the blast site, then over at the crowds of reporters.

"Move everybody back a thousand feet," Ford ordered. "Arrest anybody who argues with you."

Seamus Doyle was more than used to his boss's colorful use of bombast, and he gave as good as he got.

"You want me to arrest the firemen and the Chicago cops?" He scratched his head as if thinking it over. "Gee, boss, I don't know. I don't think they're going to like that very much."

"Nah," said Ford. "Leave the nice policemen and firemen alone. Just harass the annoying people with cameras. And give me the information."

Doyle handed his chief a handful of faxed documents, profiles of every scientist working on the Bessemer Project, complete with photographs.

Ford examined the pictures as he walked over to the small knot of scientists and tapped Shannon on the shoulder.

"James Shannon?"

"That's right."

"Thought you looked like the leader here," he said. "I'm Raymond Ford. Critical Incident

Team, FBI. I'll be running the task force on this out of the office in Washington."

A slightly concerned look crossed Shannon's face. "Running it out of Washington?"

"That's right," said Ford, reading one of the faxes in his hand. "Washington. Near Baltimore. Big city. Let's see now . . . Which one of you guys is Edward W. Kasalivich?"

Eddie stepped forward. "Me."

Ford glanced at him, then went back to his sheets of paper. "Says here you were at the lab last night. And when you got here, Professor Bucholtz was dead already. Is that correct?"

"Yeah," said Eddie. "That's right."

Ford looked at Eddie again, examining him this time, as if taking his measure. "You're sure of that fact? You're sure he was dead? Could you describe dead for me, Eddie?"

"There was a plastic bag over his head," said Eddie, his voice hoarse. "He was blue. He wasn't breathing . . ." His voice trailed off as the enormity of the death of Professor Bucholtz hit him once again.

"I'm sorry," said Ford. "I have to ask you, is there a chance he could have done it himself?"

Eddie's grief was replaced with a sharp anger. "No, there's no way," he snapped. "Yesterday was the best day of his life. Bucky worked twenty years, waiting for that day to arrive."

"Okay," said Ford evenly. "I'll take that as a no. For now anyway. Tell me, what made you say yesterday was the best day of Professor Bucholtz's life? What did he do yesterday?"

"I'll tell you exactly what he did yesterday," said Eddie hotly. "Yesterday, we—he—"

Shannon stepped up, interrupting him. "Ah, Eddie, I wonder if we could keep that under wraps for a little while longer . . ."

Ford looked at Shannon sharply. "Mr. Shannon," he said brusquely, "I already know what was going on in that lab."

"Then why did you ask Eddie?"

"I wanted to see what he said."

Doyle had finished annoying the press and returned to his boss's side. "This is Agent Doyle. I want all of you who worked in the lab to go with him to the Chicago office of the FBI."

Shannon saw his chance to make his escape. "I didn't actually work in the lab," he said. "I'm in town on business only."

"Really? Where from?"

"Washington," said Shannon.

"Now there's a coincidence, we were just talking about Washington. But, Mr. Shannon, I'd like to have you down at the office, if you don't mind." Ford turned his back on the team and started to walk away, Doyle at his side.

" 'Course I don't give a shit if he minds. Seamus, I want you to find me a friendly federal judge in the next two minutes. Shouldn't be too hard, seeing as these jokers almost gave the city the Great Chicago Fire, part two."

Doyle nodded. "Right."

"I want wiretap orders and search warrants on everyone who worked here. Understand?"

"Yes, I do," said Doyle.

"Well, you don't understand that I wanted them ten minutes ago," Ford barked, feigning anger.

"Yes I did," said Doyle grinning.

"And I want them transported in separate cars," Ford continued. "I don't want anyone working out their stories. If anyone lets them sit together they get thirty days administrative leave. Got it?"

"Only leave? You're not going to shoot 'em?" said Doyle. "You must be in a good mood."

"All right," said Ford. "Nail them with fifteen days. It's a mess."

Reporters were pushing forward, thrusting their microphones into Ford's face, hanging over the barriers as if trying to feed an animal in a zoo.

"Can you tell us why the FBI is involved?" one of them asked. Television and print reporters were just as good as cops at spotting agents of the FBI.

"Ma'am, we just had eight city blocks disappear," said Ford patiently. "I think that's a pretty good reason to get involved."

"Can you tell us—"

"Nope," said Ford, barreling through the knot of reporters. "I can't tell you a thing."

He shook off the pack of reporters and walked to his car, handing the sheaf of biographies to Doyle—all except one.

"The chemist," he said staring at it. "The Chinese guy. Chen. He was the only one missing. I want to know where he is. I want a team to move now."

Doyle did not move. Instead, he looked into the sky and rolled his shoulders as if unlimbering them. He whistled a little tune and took a gulp of fresh morning air. He did everything to suggest that he had the day off rather than that he was in the middle of a huge, top-priority investigation.

"Seamus?" said Ford. "Are you trying to annoy me? I said I want a track team on Chen right now."

"I did it already," said Doyle. "While you were sparring with the media over there."

Ford laughed and shook his head. "I may promote you someday, Seamus, you know that?"

"Yeah?" Doyle replied tartly. "You promote me, who's going to handle your job for you?"

"Just get in the car . . ."

CHAPTER TEN

The FBI floor of the Federal Building in downtown Chicago was a madhouse. All active
cases had been back-burnered to deal with the
explosion of the lab. Every agent in the office had
been recruited to interview the team scientists
and to do deep background research on every
person associated with the case.

Ford figured that Shannon was the real power
in the Bessemer Project, so he conducted that interrogation personally.

"So tell me," Ford asked. "Who are these people?" He gestured vaguely toward the outer offices where each member of Bucholtz's team sat
in a separate cubicle.

"They're scientists," Shannon said simply. "Highly trained. Experts in their various fields. A couple were graduate students working on their doctorates under Professor Bucholtz's supervision. They served as technical assistants."

"What were Bucholtz's politics?" Doyle asked. "Did you ever talk to him about that kind of thing."

Shannon shook his head. "There's nothing there," he said. "Bucky didn't give a damn about politics. He was a dreamer."

"Okay," said Ford evenly. "No politics. How about this one: who would want Bucholtz dead?"

"No one," said Shannon. "I've never heard anyone say a single word against him. Ever."

"He was a beloved figure around the old campus," said Ford sarcastically. "A regular Mr. Chips, is that it?"

"That's it," said Shannon.

"Well, someone didn't like the professor," said Ford. "After all, someone murdered him."

Interrogation of Eddie had fallen to Agents Wu and Pena. They had been over Eddie's story twice already, subtly altering their questions with each run-through. Eddie's answers, however, never varied.

"So," said Wu. "You came back for your bike."

"Yes."

"You had taken Miss Sinclair home," said Pena.

"Yes."

"Why?"

Eddie rolled his eyes. "I've told you already."

"Tell us again."

"She could not get her car started," he intoned. "And besides, she had a little bit too much to drink."

"Drinking problem?" asked Wu.

Eddie laughed. "Yesterday was the first time in her life she had ever had a little bit too much."

"How do you know that?"

"She told me."

The two agents were silent for a moment or two, staring at Eddie as if they expected him to suddenly break down and confess to the murder of Professor Bucholtz and the destruction of the lab.

"Do you have a relationship with Miss Sinclair?" Wu asked out of the blue. "Something you would like to tell us about?"

Eddie shook his head. "She's a physicist," he said.

Both agents looked a little mystified by the response. "Is there something here I'm not getting?" Pena asked.

"She's a physicist," Eddie repeated. "And I'm a machinist. Project scientists don't date machinists."

"They discriminate?" Wu asked.

"You bet they do," Eddie replied.

"So you don't know much about her?' said Pena.

"No."

"Well, tell us what you do know, Eddie," said Pena affably. "Anything, anything at all."

Eddie sighed heavily. His hands hurt now, and his head ached. His eyes were red-rimmed with lack of sleep. "She came on board a couple of years ago."

"Were you there already?"

Eddie nodded. "Yeah. I had been there about a year and a half. Only Bucky had been working on this from the beginning . . ."

"Go on."

"And he hired Miss Sinclair?" said Wu.

"Yes. No—yes, I guess."

"Make up your mind, Eddie," said Agent

Pena, an edge creeping into his voice. "What's it going to be, yes or no?"

"Well, Bucky had to sign off on every hire," said Eddie. "But Lu Chen brought her in. He met her at a conference at CalTech. Everybody was real impressed with her. She's got about six advance degrees in physics, and she speaks fluent Mandarin. That particularly appealed to Chen."

It seemed to appeal to the two agents as well. They leaned forward as if moving in for the kill.

"Did anyone else speak Chinese? Anyone else at the lab?" asked Pena. "Did Bucholtz speak it too?"

If Eddie hadn't been so tired he would have started to laugh. "No, I don't think Bucky spoke Chinese. I don't either, in case you're interested. No one else did, as far as I know."

"So Chen and Miss Sinclair could have communicated without anyone knowing what they were talking about," said Pena.

"Yeah," said Eddie. "But—"

"What was Chen's job on the project?" Wu asked.

"He was Professor Bucholtz's project manager," Eddie replied. "I guess that made him second in command."

"He was privy to everything?" Pena asked.

"Was there any part of the project that he did not have access to?"

"Man," said Eddie. "You guys are making this sound like the Manhattan Project. We all knew what was going on."

"Even you?"

"Even me."

"Did Chen ever talk about China?" Pena asked. "Ever mention how he felt about things there?"

Eddie nodded. "He sure did."

"What did he say about China?" asked Wu.

"How glad he was to be out of it," said Eddie. "The guy was crazy about the USA. He drove a Camaro, for Christ's sake. He read comic books and collected Hank Williams records. You're trying to make him out to be some kind of spy, and believe me, he wasn't."

Agents Pena and Wu exchanged glances. "After the lab exploded," said Wu, "who was the first member of your team to show up?"

"I was there already."

"After you, I mean."

"I think it was Vaclav Screbenski. He's from Czechoslovakia," said Eddie sourly. "If you want to know if he worked for the KGB, you'll have to ask him. Then everybody came pretty quickly after that."

The agents ignored the sarcasm and pushed on with their questioning. "So, within an hour, say, of the explosion every person who worked there had shown up. Is that right?"

"Except Chen," said Eddie miserably.

"Except Chen," said Wu, as if trying to make him feel worse.

"Do you have any idea where he is?" Pena asked.

Eddie shook his head slowly and looked at the two agents with poorly concealed disgust. "Have you tried his apartment?"

At that moment, the FBI trace team was standing outside the door of Chen's apartment, one of Ford's men, Caleb Williams, in charge. He gave the go signal to one of the agents, who swung a heavy sledgehammer, staving in the lock and smashing the door to splinters.

"Go! Go! Go!" yelled Williams.

The agents poured into Chen's modest apartment, high and low, guns drawn. They raced through the room, overturning furniture, upending the bed, and throwing open the closets.

The apartment was deserted. "Clear," shouted an agent in the kitchen.

"Clear!" shouted the one in the bathroom.

"Damn," said Williams. "But he was here." The room had been rifled, clothes tossed around and drawers left open. There was a suitcase on the floor. "And then he left."

"Hey! Who's gonna pay for that damn door?"

William turned and saw a middle-aged man in a set of blue overalls standing next to the wreckage of the door.

"Who are you?"

"I'm the super," the man said. He jangled the large bunch of keys clipped to his work belt. "Why didn't you just ask me for the key?"

"We were in a hurry," said Williams. "Did you know the guy who lived here? Chen?"

"Yeah," said the super. "I know all the tenants. Chen was okay. Always said hello, you know . . ."

"When was the last time you saw him?" Williams asked.

The super thought for a moment. "Ah . . . yesterday."

"What time?"

"I don't know . . . I guess it was morning. He was on his way to work. He drove a Camaro, you know."

"What do you know about his politics?"

The super got a very cagey look in his eyes. "I get it," he said. "He was pretty lefty, if you ask me."

"How do you know that?" asked Williams.

"Simple . . . he subscribed to the *New York Times*," said the super. "That's a dead give-away."

In their brief experience together, Ford had come to dislike James Shannon. He did not like his smooth demeanor. He did not like his two-thousand-dollar suit. And he particularly disliked the expensive Cuban cigar Shannon continually rolled between his fingers.

"Tell me about this Kasalivich guy," said Ford. "Pretty strange him being there right before the balloon went up."

"What about him?"

"What was his job? Was he one of your scientists, Mr. Shannon?" Seamus Doyle asked.

Shannon shook his head. "No. He's a research mechanic. Just about any project has one. He builds stuff. He works out any mechanical kinks there might be in the program. He's good at what he does."

"Was he jealous of Bucholtz?" Ford asked. "Could he have snuffed the doctor and lit the fuse? Like I say, it's pretty convenient him being there at the time, don't you think?"

"Are you out of your mind?" said Shannon. It wasn't a question asked in anger, rather it sounded as if he really did want to know the state of the FBI agent's mental health.

"I don't know," Ford replied lightly. "Am I?"

"I couldn't say. But I do know you're incorrect in following that particular line of thought. None of my people could have had anything to do with this tragedy. Particularly not Eddie."

The phone began to ring. "We'll put a pin in that, Mr. Shannon," said Ford as he reached for the telephone. "Ford . . ." He listened for a moment or two then put the receiver down on its cradle.

"Your Dr. Chen is missing," Ford told Shannon. "What do you make of that?"

"Maybe he's dead already," said Shannon, his voice full of sadness. "Maybe he was killed in the blast."

Ford nodded. "That's certainly a possibility, except he went home and packed a bag before the laboratory blew up."

It took a moment for Shannon to fathom the meaning of Ford's words. His face clouded with confusion.

"Where do you think he is?" Ford asked.

"I don't have the slightest idea," said Shannon, rolling the cigar a little more quickly.

Ford stared at him hard and wondered why he didn't light the damn thing.

CHAPTER ELEVEN

There were four television crews outside Professor Bucholtz's house, but five cameras captured Shannon, Lily, and Eddie as they walked the path cleared by the police to the front door.

"Excuse me," shouted one of the correspondents, "can we have a word with you? Did you work with Dr. Bucholtz?"

"We have no comment," said Shannon, answering for all three of them.

But that did not deter the newshounds. One of them shoved a microphone under Eddie's nose.

"I understand you were the one who found

Dr. Bucholtz in the lab. Is that correct, sir? Could we have your name?"

"I don't have any comment either," Eddie mumbled, feeling self-conscious and flustered by his sudden notoriety.

Only the wielder of the fifth camera asked no questions, and that was because the camera was mounted inside a van park a block away, the lens behind mirrored glass. It was tended by the man who murdered Bucholtz. When he caught sight of Eddie he picked up his digitally encrypted cell phone and hit speed dial.

Half a continent away, a phone beeped discreetly.

"Butler here," said the man in the van to his superior. "How do you want this thing to work?"

Butler's boss Collier chuckled. "It's simple. When the Feebies are sure they have the right man, when they're convinced they've done their little job, shoot the little bastard. Before he can say a word. Pretend you're Jack Ruby. Whack out the little patsy."

This time Butler laughed. "Jack Ruby? Ruby died in prison from eating radioactive food you and your buddies slipped him so he could never testify. I don't plan on ending that way."

Collier laughed again. Butler could not help but notice that he did not deny the charge. "Well, remember . . . Ruby got caught."

Before Butler could reply the phone went dead in his hand as Collier broke the connection. But Butler spoke anyway. "Well, of course Ruby got caught. He killed Oswald on national television, for God's sake."

The FBI had moved into Bucholtz's house big-time, crating up yards of papers and notes and removing them to the office in the Federal Building. Lily, Shannon, and Eddie looked alarmed at the ransacking.

"Hey," Shannon said, stopping one of the Feds. "We need an inventory of these things. These are very important papers."

The agent pulled away from him. "I don't know anything about that, sir. You'll have to take it up with the agent in charge."

"Ford?"

"That's the one."

Shannon knew it wasn't worth the effort. Ford would turn his request down flat.

Standing in the middle of the professor's study were a man and a woman, both in late middle age and known to Shannon personally. Eddie and Lily knew the man only by sight—he was Percy Price, the president of the University of Chicago. The woman was Bucholtz's personal attorney.

"Annette," Shannon asked the lawyer. "Can they do this? Can they take all of Bucky's research."

Annette Moore nodded and looked glum. "I'm afraid they can, James. They have a warrant. What they don't seem to have is any respect for a man's life and his work. And we can't do anything about that either."

"They have company," said Eddie. He pointed to the television that had been turned on. In the absence of any news about the blast, the local news stations had resorted to using old file footage of Professor Bucholtz. There was film of a younger version of the professor, circa 1969. His hair was longer then and he sported a tie-dyed T-shirt and Birkenstock sandals and was talking to a man dressed as the sun. Both men looked ridiculous.

"They're making him look like an idiot," Lily said sadly. "Why would they do a thing like that!"

"Then go out and tell them the truth," said Shannon. "Percy, you're the president of the university. They'll listen to you. Tell them what kind of man Professor Bucholtz was."

"I suppose I should go talk to them," said Price, walking out of the room, the lawyer right behind him.

Shannon snapped off the television set. "I have to go. I'm going to see if I can find out what the hell is going on here."

Lily and Eddie were left alone in the plundered study, a few forlorn books remaining on the shelves, light squares marking the places where Professor Bucholtz's degrees had once hung.

"What do you suppose they needed those for?" Lily wondered aloud. "Why would they take them?"

"Everything is evidence to them," said Eddie. "But it's like they erased him. Erased his life."

"I have to get out of here," Lily said. "I can't stay here."

"I have a couch," said Eddie, following her up the three flights of stairs to her room. "I could sleep on it."

"It's okay," she replied. "I can probably stay with a girl I know in the teaching fellows program."

She pulled a battered suitcase from the closet

and placed it open on the bed, but she seemed to lack the energy to open a drawer and begin to sort through her belongings. With a sigh, Lily sat down on the bed and put her head in her hands.

"I wonder if Percy Price is on television," Eddie said as he snapped on Lily's tiny TV set.

But the press was not interested in Professor Bucholtz's contributions to physics. They had something better—Ford had called a press conference and the networks had dumped their reports from Bucholtz's house to cover the FBI's briefing in the downtown office.

"We have not ruled out an accident," Ford was saying. "But our investigation is proceeding on the assumption that the laboratory was sabotaged. We have a number of leads that we still have to look over."

The instant he stopped speaking the entire press corps began shouting questions. Ford raised his hands helplessly against this onslaught, so he picked the reporter closest to him.

"Do you suspect foreign or domestic terrorism?" he shouted.

It was a question on everyone's mind. The press was so interested in the blast because they sensed that they had another Oklahoma City bombing on their hands, or at the very least, a stepped-up campaign by the Unabomer.

"We are presuming nothing at this stage of the investigation," said Ford. "However, we are asking your help in locating a man connected with the laboratory, but who is missing."

Rachel Fine placed a blown-up picture of Lu Chen on an easel beside her chief. The photograph was grainy and blurred, an enlarged version of Chen's university identification card.

"This is Dr. Lu Chen," said Ford. "A Chinese national working here in the United States. Please call the FBI if you have any information as to his whereabouts. Do not approach him—"

"Is he a suspect?" a reporter shouted.

Ford dodged the question. "We would like to speak to him. So any information you might have . . ."

As he spoke Lily's phone rang, and an instant later her fax machine began whirring, paper scrolling out.

Lily winced at Ford's words. "They think he did it," she said aghast. "I can't believe they think Chen killed Bucky and blew up the lab. He would never do anything to hurt Bucky or the experiment."

"This is insane," said Eddie, unable to take his

eyes off the screen. "Why would they blame him?"

"Because he looks different and he talks different," said Lily, her voice hollow. "And they need someone to blame."

The smearing of her friend and colleague seemed to galvanize her into action. She stood up, opened her closet, and started packing her clothes in the suitcase. She wondered if she would ever come back here.

She threw a few books into her bag then closed the suitcase and snapped it shut. "That's all I need."

"You got a fax," said Eddie. "Aren't you going to read it?"

Lily shrugged and tore the paper out of the machine, glancing at it with little interest. "It's probably a friend of mine at MIT. He said he was going to send me a fax of some—" Her face turned pale, and she sat down heavily.

"What?" said Eddie. "What is it?"

Silently she passed him the fax. Eddie took it and looked at the page dense with Chinese character forms.

"What is it?"

"It's from Chen," said Lily. "He wants me to

bring the rest of the information and meet me at the rendezvous in Shanghai."

"The rendezvous? What rendezvous?" For a moment, just a moment, Eddie went on full alert, wondering if she was part of the plot.

"I have no idea," she said. She snatched the fax from his hands and studied it. "But it's not from Chen. The vernacular is off—just. Chen was from Zhejiang, this is Shanghai, same general part of the country. If I hadn't spoken to Chen so much, it would have passed. It's close. It's very, very close."

She looked very scared, and her eyes were beginning to tear. She felt completely alone.

"This is serious," said Eddie soberly. "If the FBI sees this they're going to think you were part of it. You're being set up."

"I don't know you very well," she said, her voice tight and strained. "I haven't been here for that long . . . I haven't made many friends. I don't know anyone very well. My family is ten thousand miles away. I don't know what to do . . . I don't know where to go." She looked shaken, worn out by the staggering events of the last twenty-four hours. The elation of the successful experiment and the celebration that followed seemed an age away now.

Eddie took her by the shoulders and stood her up. "I'm not going to leave you," he said. "I'll trust you if you'll trust me. And the first thing we have to do is get out of here."

"Where are we supposed to go?" Lily looked bewildered.

Eddie almost laughed. "I have no idea."

CHAPTER TWELVE

Seamus Doyle did not attend the news conference conducted by his boss; he was too
busy. The moment Ford left the podium, though,
Doyle grabbed him and steered him into a va-
cant office. Doyle was usually a jovial sort, but
now he looked subdued and serious.

Ford could see in an instant that something
serious had come up. "What's up, Seamus?"

"Chen and Kasalivich," said Doyle. "It turns
out that the CIA has been tracking Chen for
months. Except they didn't know his name. They
just recognized his picture on your television
dog-and-pony show. They think he's already
gotten out of town. Fled to China."

"The CIA called us?" said Ford. "I'm impressed. I really am."

"That's nothing." Doyle handed Ford another file. "Check out the yellow sheet on Kasalivich."

Ford read the first few lines of the file quickly. "Son of a bitch! Why the hell weren't we informed of this?"

"Beats me."

"Let's go and find out." Ford hurried out, picking up the members of his team in his wake.

"Hey," said Agent Wu. "We intercepted a fax to Lily Sinclair."

"What's it say?"

"I don't know, " Wu said, holding it out. "It's in Chinese. I'll get it translated ASAP."

"What's the matter?" asked Doyle. "You don't speak Chinese? I thought you spoke Chinese."

"Sure," Wu retorted. "The way you speak Gaelic."

"Don't bother to get it translated," Ford ordered as he hurried down the hall. "We don't have the time. Get me an arrest warrant. Little Lily Sinclair just became a flight risk." He stopped at the elevator bank, smacked the button, and looked up at the lighted numbers above the elevators doors as if urging the cars to come, making them move faster by sheer will power.

"Seamus, you and the guys get over to wherever this Kasalivich lives," Ford ordered. "Turn that place upside down. I want anything incriminating brought back here and ticketed."

"Right," said Doyle. "But where are you going?"

"I'm going to go have a little chat with our friend Mr. Shannon," he said.

James Shannon was in the Chicago offices of his foundation, talking on the phone. He was angry.

"That is not much of an answer," Shannon snapped. "And I think I deserve a better explanation than that." He was silent a moment while his caller spoke. "Okay, fine. I'll be there."

As he hung up, Ford burst into the room. He looked angrier than Shannon had been.

"I just got Eddie Kasalivich's file." He slapped the file on the desk in front of Shannon. "It seems he had to leave the venerable University of Chicago for disciplinary reasons."

"So?" said Shannon. He knew what was coming next, but he was not going to make things easy for the FBI agent.

"I just found out he broke into a science lab after hours," said Ford, his eyes locked on Shannon's. "Apparently he wanted to run some kind of experiment, and he blew the hell out of the lab doing it. I mean, this is a coincidence, Lord Almighty. Another lab blows up, and it happens that we've got someone on the site who's got firsthand experience."

Shannon couldn't believe that Ford was getting so steamed about this; Eddie's explosion had been little more than a collegiate experiment that got a little out of hand. Eddie had gotten into more trouble for the actual break-in than for the damage done to the university laboratory.

"It was no big deal," said Shannon with a shrug. "Besides, it was a long time ago."

"I don't give a damn if it was in the Middle Ages," Ford said, enraged. "You knew this kid had been thrown out of school?"

Shannon nodded. "Yeah, but Bucholtz and I had him reinstated to work on the project."

"Under pressure, wouldn't you say?"

Shannon nodded again. "There was some pressure," he admitted. "But Eddie was valuable to Professor Bucholtz."

"A kid blows up a science building," said Ford skeptically, "and you don't think it's relevant?"

"He didn't blow up a building," said Shannon irritably. "It was minor structural damage, and no charges were filed. He was doing an interesting experiment. It might even have worked if he had a little more time to perfect his procedures. The professor respected that."

"Why didn't you tell us about it?" Ford demanded.

"I didn't think it was relevant."

Ford folded his arms across his chest and looked at Shannon as if he couldn't quite believe what he was hearing. "You didn't think it was relevant? You don't see some small connection here?"

"No," said Shannon.

"Try and see this from my side, Mr. Shannon," said Ford crankily. "I've got something here that just doesn't smell right. I've got a big bang in the middle of the night. I've got a professor dead. The CIA tells me this Chen guy might be involved in some kind of espionage. This Kasalivich guy has a past that makes me nervous, and now Miss Sinclair is getting faxes from the one-three-two-one area code, which I am told is the number you dial for Shanghai, China."

Shannon looked baffled. For one brief moment he thought he was in command of the situation, but now his instant of control had vanished, leaving his head spinning and a lot of questions unanswered.

"Not only that," Ford continued. "All the threads run right back to you. You got anything else you didn't think was important? Anything not important you haven't told us?"

Shannon did not say a word. There was a lot more to tell, but Ford could not be privy to any of it.

"Let's start with this foundation of yours," said Ford. "All anyone ever calls it is 'the foundation' as if there wasn't another one."

Shannon exhaled heavily. "The full name is the Angus C. and Mildred P. Moore Foundation for the Propagation of Global Understanding. It's easier to say the foundation. That's why we call it that."

"Who are Mildred and Angus?"

"Were. You can take them off your list of suspects, Mr. Ford." Shannon spoke with a little smile on his lips. "Angus and Mildred were dead rich people who wanted to use their money for some good. No crime there."

"No," Ford admitted.

"The foundation funds a lot of scientific research designed to make the world a better place for you and me," said Shannon, feigning sweetness and light. "There's nothing sinister about it. You can check it out in any directory of foundations available in your local public library. Maybe you'll even be moved to apply for a grant. We will listen to any proposals, though we do prefer to work with recognized institutions of higher learning."

"Maybe I will," said Ford. He didn't make it clear if he intended to check out the foundation or apply for a grant.

Shannon hoped he would just look them up in the directory. Though he knew that if the FBI agent chose to delve any further, the cover story was sure to stand up to scrutiny. After all, it had been designed by experts in deception.

CHAPTER THIRTEEN

Doyle and his team were impressed and a little disconcerted by Eddie's loft apartment. They were shocked at the complexity of his home workshop and amazed at the array of equipment. As they poked through the drawers and closets they found more evidence that Eddie could have made any explosive device short of a nuclear weapon.

"Jesus," said Doyle, awestruck. "What couldn't you build in here if you wanted to. If this is our guy, we could be facing some real serious problems. This guy could make himself a plane and fly all the way to China."

Pena opened a fireproof cabinet on the far side

of the workshop. "Look what I've got here," he shouted. "Gelignite, blasting powder, lignite, blasting caps. All nice and neat in their containers. OSHA would approve."

"Someone better call the Chicago bomb squad," said Doyle. "Let them handle this stuff."

Rachel Fine was deep in a large walk-in closet. "I need a second agent and a count here," she yelled. "Seamus, you better come and take a look at this. I think this might be what we're looking for."

Agent Fine was standing stock-still, her hands raised as if under arrest. She wanted her fellow agents to see where her hands were. Doyle pushed into the closet along with Wu and Williams.

"What you got, Rachel?" asked Doyle.

Fine kicked over a pile of dirty laundry. "Money," she said. "A lot of it." Stashed behind some of Eddie's dirty shirts and socks was a black bag. It was stuffed with hundred dollar bills, twenty to each nice, neat stack.

Doyle reached Ford at Shannon's office. Seamus told him quickly about the peculiar discovery at Eddie's apartment.

"Okay," said Ford. "I want 'em. Make sure it

gets on the news. I want every damn cop in the city looking for them . . . Wait a minute, I'll ask him.'' He covered the receiver with his hand and turned to Shannon. "Hey, do you know why anybody would get two hundred fifty thousand dollars in cash, stuff it in a black bag, and give it to our pal Eddie Kasalivich?"

"No," said Shannon smoothly. "I do not. Do you?"

"No, Seamus," said Ford into the phone. "Mr. Shannon says he doesn't know either."

He hung up the phone and stared at Shannon curiously. For a man running a philanthropic foundation, he certainly didn't rattle easily. At least, he didn't show it. James Shannon was glad the day was over. It had begun catastrophically and gotten progressively worse. Events had swept by him, and he had lost control of the situation. That was not good.

He pulled his rented Mercedes into the underground parking lot of the Four Seasons Hotel and turned off the engine. Shannon sat in the silence of the car for a moment, then slowly, wearily got out of the car and walked through the shadowy garage, making for the elevator.

Just before he got to the steel doors, Eddie and

Lily stepped out of the darkness directly in front of him.

"Shannon," Eddie hissed.

But the older man looked unfriendly, wary. "Tell me about the money in the bag, Eddie."

"What bag?"

"The one the FBI found in your closet, Eddie," Shannon snapped. "You know, the one with two hundred and fifty thousand dollars in cash. That bag. Remember it now?"

Nothing surprised Eddie anymore. "I don't know anything about it," he said. "How could I? It wasn't there when I left home last."

"Think hard," Shannon ordered.

"I'm done thinking hard," said Eddie.

Shannon let out a breath. "Okay. All right. I'm sorry," he said. Then he turned to Lily. "I assume you're not in secret communication with Lu Chen in mainland China. Right?"

Lily wasn't frightened anymore—now she was angry. And her anger showed on her face. "It has nothing to do with Chen," she said bitterly. "He could be in danger, if he isn't dead already. Someone should be trying to find him and help him instead of vilifying him on national TV."

"No one knows where he is," said Shannon. "The FBI says the CIA says he's in China."

"The CIA?" Eddie blurted out. "What are you talking about? The CIA? What the hell is going on?"

"I don't *know*, Eddie," said Shannon. "And let me tell you, I don't like not knowing. I'm going to find out, though. I know some people who might know the answer."

Before Eddie could ask who, Shannon changed the subject. "You know they've got half the cops in Chicago looking for you. And sooner or later they are going to find you. Do you have any money?"

Eddie smiled wryly. "You mean apart from the quarter mil?" He pulled out his wallet and flipped it open. "Yeah. I've got forty bucks."

Shannon already had his own wallet out. "That's not enough." He handed over all the cash he had. "Call me tomorrow from a pay phone. Get out of town, and do it fast. Go someplace you never go."

Eddie nodded. "Maggie's place."

"Good," said Shannon. "Go."

Lily sat at a table in the back of a bar, sipping a cup of coffee. Eddie was hunched over the pay phone on the wall nearby, but she could not hear what he was saying because the television set over the bar was blaring the local news. Abruptly, Eddie hung up and sat down at the table.

"Okay," he said. "There's an eight-fifteen train out of Union Station to Madison. I have a friend there. She'll put us up for a while." At least, he added silently, I think she will.

"You trust her?" Lily asked, taking a sip of the scalding hot coffee. "Will she think we're hardened . . . I don't know . . . spies?"

"I trust her," said Eddie. "We used to live together."

His voice trailed off as he caught a look on Lily's face—the slightest flicker of jealousy in her eyes, but it passed in a split second.

On the television set, the anchor said: "Updating our top story . . ." Pictures of Lily, Eddie, and Chen appeared on the screen. "The FBI has posted a ten-thousand-dollar reward for information leading to the apprehension and arrest of . . ."

"Oh shit," Eddie whispered. He pulled out his wallet and tossed money on the table.

"Buy two tickets," he said urgently. "Meet me at the track. Now get out of here, and keep your head down." He reached over and tucked her hair into her jacket. It was an oddly personal, rather calming gesture. Lily managed a shy smile.

"You go first," he said. "And be safe."

Lily got up and walked out of the bar, walking straight for the door, not making eye contact with anyone. Eddie watched her go and sipped his coffee, forcing himself to stay seated, although all he wanted to do was get to his feet and run out of there as fast as he could.

When a full five minutes had ticked by, he took a last gulp of the coffee and ambled out of the place as if he did not have a care in the world. As he passed the bar, a guy sitting there nursing a beer glanced at him and thought he looked awfully familiar.

CHAPTER FOURTEEN

It was rush hour, and the sidewalks of Michigan Avenue were jammed with pedestrians all headed home at the end of the working day. To Eddie, the crowded walkways were a boon and a curse. It was easy to melt into the crowd, but there were many more pairs of eyes that could spot him and alert the police. There was a chill wind blowing off Lake Michigan, so many of the commuters had their heads down and were hurrying to the cars and trains.

What Eddie did not know was that the guy who had glanced at him in the bar had followed him out onto the street. He paused in front of the bar, following Eddie with his eyes, not quite sure that he was the guy the police were after. As Eddie vanished into the crowd, the guy shrugged and started to return to the bar and his waiting beer when he spotted a police cruiser slowly rolling down Michigan Avenue.

"Hey!" he shouted to the cops, waving his arms to flag down the car. He crossed the street and stuck his head in the window and pointed down the street. In a second the lights and siren came on and the police car did a wild 180-degree turn, blasting off down the street.

Eddie heard the whoop of the siren and looked over his shoulder. He saw the cruiser and tensed, staring at the car, looking through the crowd. Butler, trailing him by a dozen yards, saw Eddie stop. Butler kept on walking. He looked like any other commuter, carrying a briefcase, making his way back to the suburbs.

The police car screeched to a halt at the curb and the two policemen jumped out, diving into the crowd.

"There," shouted one of the cops. "There he is."

Eddie broke into a run, but the clogged sidewalk left him no room to maneuver. He darted into the street, running south into oncoming traffic. He dodged taxis and buses like a broken field runner. Undeterred, the cops plunged into traffic too, chasing him down the middle of the street. In the distance Eddie could hear more sirens wailing in the night air.

Butler stopped on the sidewalk and watched, a smile on his face. "That's it. Go get 'em, boys."

There were half a dozen squad cars on the side streets, racing toward Eddie, cutting him off. He had no choice but to try and make it across the Michigan Avenue bridge, which spanned the Chicago River.

There were no cops waiting there to cut him off—they didn't have to. The Michigan Avenue bridge was a drawbridge, and it was already opening up, the two sections rising slowly. Eddie could see the bridge tender in his tower, a light shining through the glass of the big window.

Eddie did not hesitate. He slipped under the crossing arm and raced across the deck, a cop pounding after him. Eddie scrambled up the tilting incline, slipping and sliding on the slick surface, trying to dig his toes into the metal grating of the roadbed. Desperately, he scrambled across the slippery span, making for the side rail, clawing his way up the metal, using the handrail like a ladder.

The cop was right behind him. He made a grab for Eddie, just managing to clutch Eddie's left shoe. For just the briefest moment, Eddie and the cop hung together. Their eyes met.

"Come on, pal," the cop gasped. "Don't make it hard on yourself. Come on down." There was an agonized look on his face, and he fought to hold on, but he was slowly slipping. Finally his grip loosened, and he fell, sliding down the bridge and crashing to the asphalt below.

The bridge tender was staring out of the window in his tower, his mouth open, not quite able to believe his eyes.

"Hey, mister," he shouted at Eddie. "You crazy? What in the hell do you think you're doing up here? Get off my bridge." Then he reached for a long iron brake lever and yanked it hard.

Eddie continued to climb, reaching the bascule of the bridge, now eight stories above the ground, just as it shuddered to a halt. The vibration almost shook him loose. He clung to the cold steel of the bridge, looking down at the river on one side and a dozen cops on the other. All of them had their guns drawn and were bellowing at him to come down immediately.

Butler squatted by the embankment, his own

gun out, cackling to himself. "This is perfect," he whispered. "I couldn't have planned it this good." Now all he had to do was bide his time and wait for the right moment to pick Eddie off the bridge with a single, well-placed shot.

Two cops climbed the steps up to the bridge tender's cabin, throwing open the door and clambering in.

"Would you tell me what the hell is going on, officer?" the bridge operator asked. "I got traffic on this river and I got traffic on the streets. This is screwing up the whole city."

"The hell with that," growled one of the cops. "How do we get him down from up there?"

"I don't know! This never happened before." He peered out the window, looking up at Eddie.

"Can't you bring the bridge down?" asked the other cops. "Just lower the damn thing."

The tender shook his head. "No way. You start moving that thing and you're gonna shake him straight into the river."

"All right," said the cop. "Don't move it." He unclipped the radio on his belt. "Hey, where the hell is the Goddamn boat?"

"Who is that guy?" the bridge operator asked, still looking up at Eddie. "He some kinda psycho?"

"You know that big explosion this morning?" said one of the cops. "You know that lab that got blown up?"

"Yeah."

"That's the guy who did it."

Eddie held fast to his perch, freezing as the wind buffeted him as if it had a personal stake in tearing him from the bridge. As he looked up he found himself staring into the windows of the skyscrapers, now filling with spectators who suddenly found themselves with front-row seats for this unexpected drama. Eddie could see their faces washed by the blue and red lights from the police cars, fire engines, and other emergency service vehicles parked on both sides of the bridge. TV crews were beginning to set up, their shooting lights stabbing into the dark sky like searchlights. Eddie's world went white when the first powerful light hit him.

Michigan Avenue was thick with cops. On the other side of the raised roadway was the open mouth of the lower level of the bridge and, beneath that, more than 100 feet below him were the icy waters of the river. A police boat was nosing up the river, cutting to maneuvering speed as it got in position under the open bridge.

There were two divers on the fantail, both men hurriedly adjusting their fins and wet suits and testing their oxygen tanks.

The radio in the bridge tender's cabin crackled. "Marine Three Five," the captain of the police launch reported. "We're in position, and we've got the two divers ready on deck.

"Copy, Three Five," said the cop. He looked up at Eddie, brilliantly lit against the black of the sky. "All right, bring him down slowly."

When the bridge began to shudder again, Eddie was thrown off balance and almost plunged headlong over the side.

"Jesus!" he gasped, scrabbling for a handhold. The bridge was descending slowly, and he could see the police launch clearly now. No matter which way he went the police would get him in an instant—and that was assuming he survived the eight-story fall, of course.

But there was something else. Eddie heard a clang and a spark kicked up on the metal of the bridge a few feet from his perch. It was followed by another—a clang, followed by a spray of a bit of orange fire. Then there was a third—and it was closer than the other two.

"Someone is shooting at me!" Eddie yelled, more surprised than anything else. He peered over the side. It wasn't the police. "I've made a lot of enemies all of a sudden," Eddie said aloud. He had to get out of there and he had to be fast about it.

Eddie launched himself over the river side of the bridge. Even from that high up he could hear the gasps and screams of horrified spectators. Down on Michigan Avenue the cops and the crowd scattered to the side rails of the embankment to see him hit the water. But Eddie had disappeared.

There was a pole on the underside of the bridge, a supporting strut, and Eddie grabbed it, shimmying down it like a fireman, sliding the length of the rusty pipe, making for the lower level of the bridge.

"There he is!" someone shouted. Suddenly the light washed over him again, catching Eddie as he slipped on the pedestrian footbridge, sliding down the steep incline toward the grinding gears of the bridge mechanism housed in the underside of the tender's cabin. The giant gears interlocked, meshing together like the workings of a giant clock. There was no way Eddie could avoid the machinery. In a matter of seconds he would be ground meat. He fell through the dark opening and hit the greasy metal, the noise of the mechanism loud in his ears.

The word went up to the cop in the tender's tower. "Stop the bridge!"

"Stop the bridge!" the cop ordered.

The operator grabbed the brake lever and pulled it back hard. Instantly the bridge stopped moving. Cops went rushing into the machinery chamber, shining their flashlights on the black iron, but there was no sign of Eddie at all.

CHAPTER FIFTEEN

Lily collected the tickets from the booth and looked around furtively. There was no sign of Eddie, but she was horrified to see two cops walking through the main concourse, plainly scanning the crowds. Lily felt sick to her stomach when the awful realization hit her: they were looking for her. They wanted to arrest her. Her hands began to tremble, and she dropped the tickets, kneeling to pick them up as the cops passed by without giving her a second glance.

She stood again and looked around quickly, praying that she would see him coming through the crowd. But she was disappointed. "Come on, Eddie," she whispered. "Come on."

The public address system crackled. "Train one-thirty-four, making stops at De Kalb, Rockport, Beloit, Janesville, and Madison. Now boarding on Track Three. All aboard please . . ."

"Damn," Lily whispered. She didn't know what to do. It was plain to her that she couldn't go without him, but she couldn't stay in Chicago either. Her brained whirled, and she fought a rising panic by marching toward the exit, walking with a purpose she did not feel. The panic returned in an instant, the moment she saw another pair of cops coming through the entrance. Lily turned abruptly and walked toward the tunnel leading to her track.

She did not board the train. Instead she paced up and down the platform, watching the few passengers settling in their seats. Soon the platform was all but empty. A porter was working his way down along the length of the train, pulling up the steps and closing some of the doors. Lily was in an agony of indecision. Should she get on the train or not. The porter looked her over and smiled. He had seen this scene unfold many times over the years.

"Don't worry, miss," he said. "He'll show up. They always show up at the last minute. Trust me on that."

In spite of her hellish predicament, Lily laughed out loud. "Oh, you don't know him," she said.

The porter looked at his watch. "Plenty of time yet. And there are lots of seats. Wait it out. He'll come."

Ford and his team arrived at the bridge, barging through the crowds of cops and bystanders.

Ford flashed his badge at the nearest policeman. "Who's running this operation?"

"There's a sergeant up there," the cop said, pointing toward the operator's tower. "Talk to him."

Ford and the rest of the Feds pounded up the steps and threw open the door of the cabin. It was getting kind of crowded in the small room.

"Who the hell are you?"

Ford had his badge out again. "FBI, sergeant. Where is he?"

The sergeant shook his head. "Damned if I know. He was on top of the bridge, then he wasn't."

"Can we get the bridge down and find him?"

The bridge operator plainly did not think much of that idea. "If he's down there in the machine hold, he'll come out or get squashed like a bug in the gears. It's gonna really screw up my bridge too, if anybody cares."

"Nobody cares," said Ford. "What do you think, sergeant?"

"Well, which one would you choose? Come out or be squashed like a bug?" Ford asked.

"Me, I'd choose to come out. But that's just me," said the sergeant.

"Take it down," Ford ordered.

Eddie was wedged between two enormous counterweights, scarcely daring to breathe as the cops tried to squeeze through the chamber looking for him. Then he heard a voice squawking through one of the police radios.

"Everybody outta there! The bridge is going to move again."

"Oh shit," Eddie whispered.

The moment the cops cleared out, the whir and grinding of the machinery started again. Eddie squeezed out from his hiding place and lay flat on the cold concrete as the mechanism droned. Gears were spinning all around him. Some moved fast, some slow, some in an off-kilter elliptical path, some hardly moved at all. Suddenly, a solution came to him.

He grabbed a piece of pipe lying in the drainage channel and started studying the system of interlocking parts, figuring out the puzzle of the gears faster than any puzzle he had ever solved in his life.

It was cold in the room, but Eddie was sweating. "Okay . . ." He licked his lips and forced himself to concentrate. "Okay, drive gear," he said, tracing the mesh of gear. "Next comes the transfer gear, worm gear . . . step-down gear here." The machinery was beginning to retract, moving on greased tracks, filling the room. In a moment he would be squashed against the ungiving concrete walls.

Then he spotted it. "Master gear." He jammed the pipe in front of a small, slow-turning cog. As the pipe rotated into the teeth, there was a terrible groaning sound from the mechanism and the bridge lurched to a halt.

Eddie crawled through the gears, praying that the pipe would hold long enough for him to slither out of the drain and onto the lower roadway of the bridge. He emerged from the housing like a gopher and slid under the first car waiting in line to cross the bridge. No one noticed him—everyone's attention was turned to the bridge, stuck half open.

He slithered along the length of the underside of the car, the shoes of cops visible on either side of him. Clawing his way down the line of cars was not easy. The skin on his hands and knees scraped off on the asphalt. When he emerged from under the fifth car in line, he was gasping for breath, as if he had been submerged under water. His heart was beating fast and he was panting, but he forced himself to walk away calmly, doing nothing to attract attention.

The track announcer was calling the Madison train for the last time, when Eddie burst through the big main doors of Union Station.

Lily was just about to give up, stepping onto the lower stair of the train when Eddie came racing down the platform. She sagged with the relief of seeing him, helping him on board just as the train started to move.

"What took you so long?"

But Eddie could only shake his head, too exhausted to find the words to explain what had happened.

Ford stormed around the bridge platform, ranting to his staff and to anyone else who cared to listen to his passionate bitching.

"The entire Chicago police force," he yelled. "The FBI, boats, scuba divers and we couldn't get him! What the hell is this? He's a kid. He's a *machinist*!" He shook his head and stared at the ground. "Dogs . . . Maybe if we had dogs we would have been able to catch him."

Doyle waited patiently until he had a chance to speak. "Are you just venting there, boss, or do you really want me to get a pack of blood-hounds?"

Ford considered the idea for a moment. "Naww," he said finally. "You can put a hold on the dogs. Maybe some other time." He rubbed his chin and stared up at the bridge as if expecting to see Eddie up there again. "I'd pay to find out how he slipped away like that."

"Maybe he mashed up inside the gear housing and they just haven't found him yet," Caleb Williams suggested. "Maybe he stopped the bridge with his femur or something."

"No, he's gone," said Ford. "If he had been ripped up by the machinery we would have known. Think about it. Could you die silently if that was the way you went? I couldn't."

"You know," said Doyle, "the trouble with dogs is if they get out of hand on you, you can't just go ahead and shoot 'em. If you do, the ASPCA really gets on your case about it."

"I hate that," said Ford.

"I do have some good news . . ." said Doyle.

"Give it to me," growled Ford. "I need it bad."

"Mr. Shannon is leaving town," Doyle reported. "He has himself a ticket on the early flight tomorrow morning. O'Hare to National Airport, Washington. He's got an office there."

"So do we," said Ford. "I want a plane."

CHAPTER SIXTEEN

The air in Madison was clear, clean, and cold, and the little town bustled even though it was close to midnight by the time Eddie and Lily disembarked from the train. There were still University of Wisconsin students on the streets or hanging out at the various bars and clubs that catered to the college population.

But Lily and Eddie hardly noticed the kids, they were still shell-shocked by all that had happened to them that day. They grabbed a cab outside the station, the driver taking them across the campus and on to the edge of town.

The Yerkes Observatory was a distinctive domed building set on a small rise. The viewing port was open, and a portion of the big refracting telescope could be seen poking through the aperture like the barrel of an artillery field piece.

"Built in 1897 and still going strong," said Eddie. "There's only one other like it in the world."

"Did you go to school here?"

"Oh," said Eddie. "I audited some courses here . . ." He started up the steps to the observatory.

"Is your friend going to be here this late?" she asked. "I mean, won't she be surprised?"

"Don't worry about it," said Eddie. "It takes a lot to surprise Maggie. She's kind of wild. She's generally up all night anyway."

Lily grimaced slightly, but Eddie missed it. Great, she thought, she was just about to meet some wild machinist babe he used to be with. She prepared herself for a girl with a lot of tattoos and probably a stud in her eyebrow.

The huge, round main room of the observatory was dominated by the immense 120-inch telescope. Eddie walked right in as if he knew his way around the place.

"Maggie! Maggie!" His voice echoed in the enormous room. "Where are you? You here tonight?"

"Up here." Maggie McDermott stood at the top of the viewing platform twenty or thirty feet up the length of the telescope. As she clambered down the stairs, Lily got something of a shock— the astronomer was not a wild-looking chick but a serene-looking woman in her middle sixties. She was bundled up against the cold, but Lily guessed she did not have a single tattoo or piercing.

Maggie stopped a few feet from Eddie and looked him over, shaking her head like a slightly disapproving aunt. Then she enfolded him in a warm, prolonged hug. "Oh, Eddie," she said. "You've gotten very famous very quickly." She held him out at arm's length. "Tell me you didn't do it."

"I didn't do it," said Eddie.

She looked at him for one more moment, just to be sure. "Okay," she said. "I'm sure."

Maggie turned to Lily. "And you must be the other terrorist I've been hearing so much about," she said.

"Maggie has what is known as a dry sense of humor," Eddie explained. "You have been warned."

"I'm sorry," said Maggie, smiling. Then she hugged Lily warmly. "Any friend of Eddie's . . .

Come into my office. It's warmer there."

Lily had been in hundreds, perhaps even thousands of offices like Maggie's in universities and institutions all over the world. It was crammed with books, the old wooden desk buried under an avalanche of more books, papers, and academic journals. Even the tea Maggie brewed up and the cookies she offered from a dented round container seemed to be the same served in every professor's office from Rome to Reykjavik.

Suddenly, she was filled with a great sense of sadness. All she wanted was to return to her safe, secure nest in academia. But she had a feeling that she had been ejected from that world already. She tried to drive the melancholy from her mind, sitting up straight and sipping her tea.

"Eddie said you used to live together," said Lily. "Was that here in Madison, or what?"

And like all those professors in their messy offices the world over, Maggie seemed to have some sort of psychic filing system that allowed her to put her finger on any object, book, or paper in the jumble that appeared to have no formal order. Maggie pulled a photograph from the middle of a pile of papers and handed it to Lily.

It showed Maggie and Eddie standing together, both of them dressed in heavy, hooded coats, standing in the middle of a stark snow-scape. Both were grinning at the camera.

"Eddie and I used to live together in the South Pole station," Maggie explained. "You don't know how much you love your mechanic until you find out he knows how to fix the only toilet within twelve hundred miles."

"When he said you lived together, I imagined something else." Lily took another sip of her tea. "Professor—"

"Maggie."

"Maggie, I hope we're not interrupting your work," she said apologetically. "I know how frustrating that can be."

"The universe will still be there tomorrow, dearie," said Maggie kindly. "But Bucky . . . I'm going to miss him."

"You knew him?"

"I spent six months in the South Pole with him too, honey," Maggie replied, a soft smile on her lined face. "And he was a little closer to my age, you know. That was some trip, wasn't it, Eddie?"

"Sure was," Eddie said. "It was pretty excit-ing."

"I remember Bucky told me he had a plan to

save the world," said Maggie. "All he needed was the money and the time to put his theories to the test. Was there anything to it? How close was he when he died?"

"We had achieved a fully sustainable burn on the last test," said Lily. "We generated one-point-two times the energy we were putting in. He was there. He had done it." She shook her head sadly. "It's hard to believe that was just last night. Twenty-four hours ago we were drinking champagne and celebrating."

Maggie was silent for a long time. When she spoke again, her voice was unsteady. "Good God," she said gently. "He did it. Bucky finally did it. That Goddamned idealist." Then Maggie McDermott began to cry, grieving for her old lover and her lost friend.

James Shannon's flight from Chicago touched down right on time, bright and early, at National Airport in Washington D.C. He retrieved his sleek silver Jaguar from the long-term parking and drove out of the city, making for Virginia and the exclusive area north of the city centered on the rich little town of McLean.

Shannon may have arrived in Washington early, but Ford and his group had gotten there ahead of him. As he drove down a quiet country road on the outskirts of McLean, he paid no attention to the cable TV van parked on the shoulder, two workmen installing a line. Had he looked closer, he would have noticed that the two linemen were FBI agents Wu and Pena and that they had installed a line-of-sight video transmitter behind a telephone transformer, the powerful lens trained directly on Shannon's home.

The tall wrought-iron gates swung open, and the Jaguar glided up the long driveway towards the large, elegant Georgian mansion set in the middle of the five or six acres of perfectly maintained garden.

In the command center of the Critical Incident Task Force, Ford and Doyle watched as Wu adjusted the lens of the camera. Ford picked up a headset and slipped it on.

"What you got out there?"

"We got Mr. Shannon where he lives and breathes," Wu replied. "Nice spread, huh?"

The estate suddenly came into sharp focus on Ford's screen. "That's very nice real estate," he said.

"I think I should give up this line of work and become a philanthropist like Shannon. The pay looks pretty good," said Seamus Doyle. "I guess when you're in the business of giving away money some of it just happens to get stuck in your own bank account."

Shannon stayed at his house long enough to hand his luggage over to his manservant and change his clothes. Then he returned to the Jaguar.

"He's on the move again," said Pena into his headset.

"Stay with him," Ford ordered. "Shadow cars roll now. Let's make sure Mr. Shannon has company but not so he notices."

There was a whole squad of characterless government cars scattered around Loudoun County, ready to follow Shannon for a few miles before handing off to another car. No one vehicle—except for a helicopter flying at high altitude—would follow Shannon all the way to his destination. If the system worked, Shannon would never have the slightest idea that he was being tailed.

But first he threw the Feds a curve. They had made the mistake of assuming that Shannon would head east toward Washington D.C. Instead, he turned west toward Winchester, Virginia, then south to Front Royal at the head of the Shenandoah National Park and the Blue Ridge Mountains.

It was a long and rather beautiful drive, but neither Shannon nor his followers were much in the mood for sightseeing. Ford sat in his office, glancing at the TV monitor from time to time while he and Doyle worked their way through two piles of dossiers, one stack labeled THE ANGUS C. AND MILDRED P. MOORE FOUNDATION, the other JAMES SHANNON.

"Where the hell is he going?" Ford wondered aloud.

"Maybe he got a yen to take a ride down Skyline Drive," Doyle answered. "It's nice. You should try it some time."

"How come I have the feeling you haven't guessed right on that one, Seamus?" Ford asked.

The speaker squad box on Ford's desk crackled. It was the observer in the helicopter. "He's turned off the main road," he said.

The camera in the belly of the chopper swiveled to follow the silver Jaguar, zooming for a tight shot on a security checkpoint. Shannon's car just rolled by the guard without stopping, giving as ID only the most casual of waves. He continued up the road to a small red brick building, something out of the 1950s institutional architecture workbook. He parked his car and disappeared into the structure, blithely unaware that he was being observed.

Ford leaned forward to get a better view of the screen. "You know, Seamus," he said. "That's an awfully small building, and there sure are a hell of a lot of cars in that parking lot."

Wu and Pena got into position on a low bluff overlooking the guard post and the gate to the property Shannon had just entered.

"Boys and girls," said Ford. "I want every license plate. Anything going in, anything going out, and any you can see in the parking lot . . ."

There was a heavily armed guard on the desk inside the building, but he wore no uniform or badge or any other type of insignia.

"Welcome back to Weather Mountain, Mr. Shannon," the guard said. "Sign in, please."

Shannon signed, crossed the lobby of the silent building, and stepped into a huge elevator, a cabin larger than any freight car. He slipped a key into a slot and turned it—there was no control panel, because the huge elevator only had two destinations. Top—where Shannon was— and the bottom, where he was going.

The elevator dropped 1,200 feet, down the

shaft that had been carved from the rock of the mountain.

The steel doors swept open and Shannon stepped out, entering what appeared to be a small town buried deep underground. Large corridors had been hacked from the granite, the ceilings lined with electrical, ventilation, and communications ducts that snaked through the passages. The walkways were thronged with people, some wearing white lab coats, all of them looking as if they were very busy and had to get to their destinations as quickly as possible. No one gave Shannon a second glance, which was just fine with him.

The man Shannon had come to see had the largest, most luxurious office in the Weather Mountain complex, but it was difficult to see any details. The room was dimly lit, and he sat in the shadows watching the array of computer screens in front of him, financial data from a dozen different markets around the world.

"Sell the platinum, sell it now," Collier murmured into the phone. "Dump it all." He chuckled, bemused by the thought of his own extraordinary business acumen.

He hit a button on his desk and all the computer screens winked and went blank. "Come in, James," said Collier. "Take a seat."

Shannon sat in the soft, cool leather chair that faced Collier's wide, ebony desk. Collier controlled three-quarters of a billion dollars in black budgets, and Shannon was sure that the pressure and power of his situation had driven John Collier the tiniest bit crazy.

"So," said Collier mischievously. "What's new? Anything interesting going on up on planet earth?"

James Shannon was in no mood for small talk, fooling around, or playing mind games with his superior. "John, would you like to tell me what the fuck is going on? I have to know."

Collier got serious quickly. "The long and the short of it is you had a leak in your setup, James. That's bad."

"Who?"

"Chen. He didn't start out bent, though," said Collier. "We think the Chinese government had Chen's family back in Shanghai. They put the squeeze on him, and he broke."

Shannon absorbed this information without a flicker of emotion. "When? When did they turn him?"

"Hard to tell right now," Collier replied. "We

have to assume that it was early on in his tenure."

"Who else?"

"Well, this Lily Sinclair was obviously a part of it. He needed someone who spoke English and Chinese, and he did bring her aboard," said Collier. "Again, we have to assume she is tainted." Collier cracked his knuckles. "And we think she turned Eddie Kasalivich."

"Impossible," said Shannon. The word was so clipped it sounded as if he had bitten it off his vocabulary.

"How can you be so sure?" Collier asked. "Because you were close to him? Lily Sinclair may have gotten closer, if you know what I mean. It wouldn't be the first time that a recruit was made between the sheets."

"I hired him," said Shannon. "I knew him. He would not have sabotaged the experiment. He would never have dreamed of killing Professor Bucholtz. I know that for sure."

Collier considered this for a moment. "Well, I suppose . . . We're checking on him, James. It could be that they set him and the guy up. Planted the money and faked the fax to the girl."

Now Shannon looked puzzled. "Why? Why go to all that trouble to set up two pawns?"

"Because they were pawns?" said Collier. "I'm guessing they set this whole thing up to hide Chen. I don't have to tell you we are in a very sensitive situation with the Chinese government here. Hell, they've already as good as threatened to nuke Los Angeles if we don't butt out of Taiwan."

Shannon leaned forward. "Well, fuck the Chinese, John. You're usually the first one to say that. Right after you've said fuck the Russians. And the Germans. And the Japanese. Am I leaving anyone out?"

"The British," Collier prompted. "Don't forget I usually say fuck the British right after I say fuck the Russians."

Shannon did not think that was in the least bit funny. He was so angry he felt as if he was about to go into orbit. "Look at me, John," he said incensed. "Look at me closely. Do you see two big round objects and a pink, puckered eye in the middle. Do I look like an asshole to you?"

He stood up and leaned on the desk, getting right up in Collier's face. "I've been in this business twenty-five years. The Chinese? Lu Chen? What do you take me for? I'm not an amateur. You didn't honestly think I would fall for some second-rate cover story like that, did you? Christ, John. That's offensive."

For a moment Collier thought about sticking to his story, toughing it out. But he changed his mind.

"Well," he said philosophically. "It was worth trying. You might have bought it." Collier shrugged. "Who knows . . ."

"I wouldn't have bought that, not in a million fucking years." Shannon dropped back into his chair. "I told you, I have to know what's going on here, John. So cut the crap and tell me."

"Okay, no bullshit, James . . . It was you. Your fault."

"Me?" Shannon almost yelped the word. "What the hell are you talking about now? Bessemer ran perfectly."

"You didn't control your people, James."

"That's bullshit."

"Really?" Collier replied. "Did you know that Bucholtz was going to put his data out on the Internet that night, right after he ran the experiment? It would be all over the world now if we hadn't stopped him."

"He wouldn't have done that," said Shannon, suddenly subdued. "I talked to him about it. He told me he would not do that."

"He lied," said Collier. "We needed to stop him and we needed to discredit the hydrogen technology. Television has been all over this like a cheap suit—they like the pictures of smoking ruins and bomb craters a few miles from the Loop. It makes everybody good and scared.

"Right now it looks like we've set back hydrogen-based energy technology by at least fifteen years," said Collier gleefully. "And we have all of Bucholtz's research data. We're not stupid. We got everything before we blew it up. The whole thing has been rebuilt down here."

Shannon shook his head. "You really screwed me, John. Big time. And it's all so unnecessary..."

"There just one problem," said Collier.

"Now there's an understatement," Shannon snapped. "I'd say we have more than one little problem."

"You may have more than one problem," Collier corrected him. "You may have a bushel basket full of problems. I don't care about that. I mean, down here we have a little problem. We have all of Bucholtz's specs and data, we have people as good as or better than the ones working in Chicago... But they can't get the damn thing to work."

Shannon laughed out loud. "Now that's funny."

"Really?" said Collier sourly. "You want to tell me why that's so damn funny? You ask me, it's a catastrophe."

"I'm not going to tell you," said Shannon, toying with him. "Not yet, anyway. Tell me, why did you decide to pin this thing on Eddie Kasalivich? What did he ever do to you?"

"It was nothing personal," Collier said, shrugging. "Your pal Eddie just had the bad luck to walk in on Bucky and he was just an idiot machinist that no one gave a damn about, so who cared?"

Shannon laughed again. "You better call off the FBI and the marshals and the Coast Guard and the Texas Rangers and the Cub Scouts and whoever the hell else you have looking for him and the girl."

"Very funny," said Collier. "Its just the Bureau. And they have to find him, because we need someone to pin this on."

"Well, I wouldn't choose Eddie, if I were you." Shannon spoke seriously this time. "You would be making a terrible mistake."

"I can't call them off," Collier replied. "We'd

have a lot of explaining to do. I'm not sure it can be done."

"You might try," Shannon insisted.

Collier peered at him through narrowed eyes. "Are you just sticking up for him because he's your boy, or is it something else? What makes some Joe Six Pack machinist worth going up against the FBI."

"Because that Joe Six Pack, John," said Collier evenly, "is the guy who made the experiment work. He supplied the last piece. He built it by hand. You can comb through all the disks and manuals you want, but you'll never find it because the specs were never recorded. Eddie is the only one on the planet who knows how to make your precious machine perform miracles."

For a moment John Collier's mask of icy calm slipped and he looked flabbergasted. But he recovered quickly.

"Fine," he said. "We have an advantage then. One that we should exploit to the limits."

"What's that?"

"Eddie trusts you. And you're on our side," Collier replied. "Go and get him back."

CHAPTER
SEVENTEEN

On the second floor of the student union building of the University of Wisconsin was a long, airport-style bank of pay phones—fifty or more of them in a long line. Few of them were in use at that early hour of the morning.

Maggie McDermott was speaking on one of them, Eddie and Lily hovering nearby, newly attired in clothes left behind by Maggie's ever-changing group of transient house guests. They wore warm parkas that zipped to the chin and hoods they could pull down almost over their eyes, and both Eddie and Lily wore well broken-in, but stout and sturdy hiking boots on their feet. They were refreshed after a good night's sleep and a hot meal, both of them ready to make an attempt to unravel the web of mysteries in which they were enmeshed.

The secretary in Shannon's Chicago office answered the phone. "Mr. James Shannon, please," said Maggie.

"I'm afraid he's not here," the secretary replied. "Whom may I say is calling?" The woman was polite but far from friendly.

"My name is Maggie McDermott . . ."

"And does Mr. Shannon know what this is in reference to?"

"I was a friend of Doctor Bucholtz," Maggie replied. "I have something of his here. Something I think Mr. Shannon would like to have."

Bucholtz's name acted like a spell on the secretary. The icy demeanor melted in an instant. "Mr. Shannon is in Washington, Ms. McDermott. Would you like me to transfer the call?"

"Yes, please . . ."

Caleb Williams was on the wiretap watch that morning, monitoring all calls into and out of Shannon's offices. He logged in the call, writing down Maggie's name and the time of the call. Then the agent swiveled in his chair and tapped a few buttons on a computer keyboard, activating the trace. He followed the switching stations as it jumped back along the route of the call.

"Okay," said Williams. "Not a local call . . . Not Illinois . . ." In a matter of seconds the computer traced the call to a number in Madison, Wisconsin, and a second later it digested that number and spat out the exact location. Still, it was no big deal to Williams. Maggie McDermott was not on any watch list, she was just some old lady calling Shannon.

More out of boredom than anything else, he continued to listen to the call. "Moore Foundation," said the secretary in Washington. "Mr. Shannon's office."

"James Shannon, please," said Maggie diffidently. "Maggie McDermott calling. I need to talk to Mr. Shannon about Professor Bucholtz."

The call was transferred instantly to Collier's office, where Shannon took the call. "Professor McDermott? I understand you were a friend of Dr. Bucholtz's."

But Maggie did not speak. She handed the phone to Eddie. "Shannon, it's me," he whispered.

Caleb Williams nearly jumped out of his chair the instant Eddie's voice sounded down the line.

He smacked down on the intercom that connected his office with Ford's.

"Boss? I just picked it up, Kasalivich is in Madison, Wisconsin. He's talking to Shannon right now."

"Christ! I'll be right there."

Ford came barreling into the room followed by Doyle. "Caleb, call the Bureau office in Madison, get them to hook up with the locals."

"Eddie?" said Shannon. The surprise in his voice was very obvious. "Is that you?"

"Yeah."

"Don't say another word," Shannon ordered. He slammed down on a switch mounted on a box next to the phone, a high-pitched whine splitting the FBI office like a buzz saw as the scrambler kicked in.

"Scrambled," said Williams. "Damn it!"

"Hey, haven't you heard? A lot of charitable organizations use fully encrypted digital communication," said Doyle. "It's so UNICEF doesn't listen in and go out and hog all the good donations . . ."

"Okay, Eddie," said Shannon. "You can speak now."

"Good . . ."

"Are you okay?" Shannon asked.

"Yeah . . . considering."

"I understand," said Shannon. "Are you where you said you'd be?"

Eddie hesitated for a moment, but then he told himself that he had no option but to trust Shannon. "Yeah, I'm there," he said finally.

"I need to help you," said Shannon earnestly.

Lily elbowed Eddie hard in the ribs and pointed to the entrance of the building. Two police cruisers and an unmarked car had screeched up to the curb in front of the student union.

"Eddie . . . ?" said Shannon. "I want you to stay where you are. I'm going to send someone to pick you up."

"Can't do that," said Eddie hurriedly. "Can't stay here. I'll come to you." He put the phone down, but did not hang up. Shannon could hear very little, and he was in a lather of frustration.

"Eddie? Eddie? Shit." He pressed his ear to the phone. He could make out a siren and prayed he did not hear gun shots.

Eddie and Lily pulled the drawstrings of their hoods tight and wrapped scarves around their necks. Maggie was watching, looking out into the forecourt of the building. Even more cop cars were drawing up.

Lily took Eddie by the hand. "Come on," she said. "Let's go."

"There's nowhere *to* go," said Eddie.

"Yes there is," said Lily. "We have a bus to catch." She marched out of the door, dragging Eddie behind her.

The parking lot of the student union was the focal point for the various school outings organized by the student clubs. On the way in, Lily had spotted one organization, the Young Republicans, pulling skis out of a snowbank and loading them into the cargo bay of an excursion bus.

Lily led Eddie to the ranks of skis sticking out of the snow. "I don't know what your politics are," she whispered through her scarf. "But don't look now, you just became a Young Republican."

"I love them," said Eddie.

Looking supremely self-assured, Lily yanked a pair of Rossignol skis out of the snowbank and marched over to the waiting bus. She threw the skis into the luggage compartment and waved to Eddie.

"Come on, hon!"

"I like her," Maggie whispered in his ear. "Go."

Eddie grabbed "his" skis from the snow and

did as Lily had done, walking on to the bus with a quick wave to Maggie.

"Okay," said the driver. "That's a full load." The door closed with a sharp pneumatic hiss. As Eddie looked back he could see Feds and cops swarming into the student union building. Not one of them thought to check the bus.

"They got away!" Ford thundered. "They got away again? How in hell did that happen?"

Doyle shook his head. "We should have gotten those dogs, chief," he said. "Shoulda gone with your gut instinct."

Ford turned on him, his face dark with anger. For a moment, Doyle blanched, afraid that maybe this time he had gone too far. But the moment passed, Ford deciding not to waste his time losing his temper. The task he had at hand was much more important.

"Search the whole area," Ford shouted. "I want them found. And I want them found to-day!"

Peter Wu came running into the command center, a roll of fax paper in his hands and a puzzled look on his face. "Boss, all those plates you wanted run, the ones from the place in the hills . . ."

"Yeah?"

"None of them exist."

Ford looked at him hard. "What about the place you were at, the place Shannon went? Maybe that doesn't exist either."

"No, it doesn't. There is no record of that building, not on the county rolls. It's not even on the map."

"Maybe you weren't really there."

"That would be one explanation," Doyle put in.

Ford scooped up a pile of files on the Moore Foundation. "But I'll bet there are probably others too."

CHAPTER EIGHTEEN

James Shannon was not in the slightest bit surprised when his manservant entered his study and announced that two gentlemen from the FBI were here to see him. The man betrayed nothing, maintaining his aplomb absolutely; he had long ago gotten used to his employer's peculiar movements and even more peculiar guests.

Ford walked in, glaring at Shannon. He slapped the fat file on the Moore Foundation down on the desk.

"I knew we'd be meeting up again some day," said Shannon, smiling that shadowy little smile of his.

"Well, it just so happens that I found another one of those unimportant pieces of information of yours . . ."

"Oh dear," said Shannon lightly.

Ford thumped the file with his fist. "This is the Moore Foundation's file from the Internal Revenue Service."

"Really?" Shannon leaned forward and peered at it as if it was some rare piece of flora. "And here I always thought that tax records were supposed to be confidential. Silly me."

"Silly fucking naive little you, Shannon," Ford rasped. "Should I tell you what's in the Moore Foundation IRS file?"

"Well, we are a nonprofit organization," Shannon replied. "So I would guess that it contains rather meager tax records."

Doyle nodded. "He's good," he said. "That was a good answer, you have to admit."

Ford dropped into a chair facing Shannon. His anger appeared to have vanished completely. "It's interesting. The funding for this foundation of yours seems to come from a wide variety of sources. But all the checks end up coming from the same bank. From the same account. And that information is classified. Why do you suppose that is, Mr. Shannon?"

Shannon shrugged. "I couldn't say. I don't do the accounting, of course. Plus, as you mentioned, it's classified. So, even if I knew, I would not be at liberty to tell you about it."

"That was a good one too," said Doyle.

Ford tossed another file on the first. "Know what that is? That's your resume. Very impressive . . . You Yale boys, you go so far in life. But it leaves out one important thing."

"Which is?"

"Which is who pays your salary," said Ford.

"The Angus C. and Mildred P. Moore Foundation pays my salary," said Shannon smoothly. "I thought I mentioned that."

Ford nodded. "Now this is where things get really interesting. I have a friend at Langely who tells me that they pay your salary. What do you make of that, Mr. Shannon?"

"Well, that *is* interesting," said Shannon affably. "I'll definitely have to look into that myself. Maybe the elusive foundation accountant would know more about my source of income."

"Ha-ha," said Doyle.

"A man might be forgiven for concluding that your precious foundation is a front for the people at Langley as well," said Ford meditatively. "Mr. Shannon, do I need to tell you that interfering with an FBI investigation is a federal crime. It is a very serious offense."

Shannon was only too happy to parry. "I know the law, Mr. Ford," said Shannon. "And I know the penalties as well. If, however, this was a front for the people at Langley, you just might be treading on national security issues here. A man who stuck his head into something like that just might find it cut off."

Ford nodded, more than happy to play along. "Maybe you would like to share a little information with us."

"Such as . . . ?"

"Such as another little bit of insignificant information, such as what the hell is going on here?"

"Mr. Ford . . ."

"That's Agent Ford."

Shannon raised his hands lightly, as if waving off the correction. "All the other stuff aside, if I knew I would tell you."

Ford leaned forward, until he was almost nose-to-nose with Shannon. The agent had dropped his air of false bonhomie. "I hope so, Mr. Shannon. 'Cause these people are suspects in a crime of murder and massive destruction of public property. Possibly espionage."

"I am thankful that does not concern me, *Agent* Ford."

For a moment Doyle was afraid that Ford was going to reach out and haul Shannon across the desk by his Hermes foulard tie, but his chief managed to control himself.

"I know the law too," Ford snarled. "And no national security case sanctions murdering people—not domestically at least. What happens in Asia, Africa, Central America, well, I don't give a damn about that. Maybe you are telling the truth, Mr. Shannon. Maybe you really don't know what's going on. But remember, your friends at Langley are not allowed to play here. Domestic is my backyard."

He gathered up his folders and headed for the door. "Don't screw up on my playground," he called over his shoulder. "Believe me, you really don't want to do that."

The police in Madison, Wisconsin, had managed to lift a set of partial fingerprints from the pay phone and matched them to a fax of Eddie's prints that had been sent from Washington.

Police were conducting a sweep through the student union center and the area surrounding, checking every room, public and private, running checks on every vehicle in the parking lot, questioning bystanders, checking identification. Students were standing around in groups, watching the frenzied but pointless activity of the police.

Two of the undergraduates, however, had other things on their minds. They were standing in the parking lot, staring at the holes in the snow where their skis used to be.

"They were right here," said the young man. "Right here. Someone stole my skis. I can't believe it. Animals. Who would do a thing like that? They were new Salomons. Brand new. My dad is gonna kill me."

"I knew we shouldn't have stopped for coffee," said his girlfriend. "We should tell the cops. There are like fifty of them here."

The skier and the girl walked over to a knot of cops and FBI agents. "Excuse me, officer?"

The policemen and the Feds turned. "Yeah?"

"Someone stole our skis," said the girl.

"Who?"

"I don't know," said the boy. "If I knew, they wouldn't be stolen. And they took our seats on the bus."

"Bus?" asked one of the uniformed policemen.

"Yeah, for the ski trip, up at Lake Howe

Lodge," the girl put in. "Can you do something about this? We are really bummed . . ."

All the cops and Feds exchanged glances rapidly. They were all wondering the same thing: could it be? Could it be that simple? In an instant they all agreed—once in a while you *could* get lucky. Things *could* be that simple. And they *could* do something about it.

The Young Republican ski trip bus rolled up to the ski lodge three hours after leaving Madison, and Eddie for one had never been so glad for a journey to end. There had not been two seats together, so Eddie had been forced to sit next to some very young, very Republican economics major who had held forth on arcane conservative economic theories all the way up into the mountains. By the time they finally arrived, Eddie felt as if he had been bored until he turned to lead.

As they disembarked from the bus the economist tapped Eddie on the shoulder and offered a piece of advice in parting.

"Remember," he said. "Debt management and military spending. That's what made this country great."

"Thank God that's over," Eddie mumbled to Lily.

"I didn't speak to anyone. I napped all the way," she stretched deliciously and drank in the sunshine and the sweet air.

"That's great . . . for you," Eddie grumbled.

"Well, maybe we've bought some breathing room. Maybe we can slow down a little, get something to eat . . ."

But Eddie was not paying attention. He was staring down the road they had just come up. Lily stopped speaking and followed the line of his gaze. Way, way off in the far distance they could see the frantic red and blue strobe lights of the approaching police cars.

"What do we do now?"

"Run like hell," said Eddie. "Come on."

Together they ran around the side of the ski lodge and stumbled toward the lake that gave the resort its name. Lake Howe was large but frozen solid and covered with snow at this time of year. Ice fishermen dotted the surface, their huts dark smudges on the white snow. Here and there graceful ice boats carved tracks across the frozen surface. They would have considered it a very pretty little scene—if they hadn't been running for their lives.

They could hear the sirens now. Vacationers, fishermen, and lodge staffers were beginning to turn and look as the cavalcade of wailing cop cars blasted up the hill to the lake.

"Oh shit." Eddie grabbed Lily by the wrist, and they pounded down the slope to the lake shore, then out onto the frozen water.

"Where are we going?"

"I don't know."

A hundred and fifty yards out on the lake an ice boat soared by. They could hear the wind luffing in the sail and hear the blades of the runners slicing through the ice. The skiff was probably twenty-five or thirty feet long with a forty-five-foot mast. The vessel was so light and put out such a volume of canvas that it could hit speeds of sixty miles per hour or greater.

Lily thought she had found the solution. "Do you know how to sail one of those things?"

"No," said Eddie.

Lily grimaced. "I was sort of getting used to your being able to do anything, you know."

As she spoke, the ice boat tried to come about. The boom swung in a vicious arc, the canvas billowed, and the blades on the right side pulled up off the ice, the whole vessel capsizing at high speed. The ice boat took a long, vicious slide across the ice, the mast coming down in a tangle of rigging, the pilot tossed high in the air and hitting the hard ice with an audible thump.

"Well . . . no loss," said Lily.

A contingent of police was coming down onto the ice, running to each ice fishing hut, stopping everybody, checking identification.

"We have to get across the lake," said Eddie, "get in the woods on the far side, and get under cover."

A group of policemen were trudging toward them now, shouting for them to stop. Lily and Eddie did the opposite, running for the shore, falling in the deep snow. Behind them they heard the amplified voice in a loudhailer.

"Stop where you are and put your hands up."

Lily and Eddie kept running. The sound of the bullhorn was augmented by a more ominous one. A ski mobile screamed into life and started blazing across the frozen surface of the lake, throwing up snow in its wake.

They crashed into the dense wood on the other side, climbing the steep bank, trying to get as deep as possible into the forest. As they scaled the slope, Lily lost her footing and tumbled into a little gully carved in the snowy hillside by a creek that fed into the lake. She crashed through the ice and into the frigid water. It wasn't deep, scarcely up to her knees, but she fell heavily, the down in her parka soaking up the freezing water.

Eddie yanked her up by the collar of her sodden coat and pushed her up the slope again, throwing her flat into a snowdrift as a helicopter clattered by overhead, flying at a height a few feet off the tree tops. The noise was deafening for a moment, then it abated, leaving them deep in the hush of the forest.

"I don't think they saw us," he said, gulping for air. "It's okay. I think it's safe now."

Lily was shivering violently, her teeth chattering. "I'm freezing," she stammered. "God, it's cold."

"We have to keep moving," he said.

"I thought you said we're safe here." Suddenly she looked very tired. Fatigue was always the first stage of hypothermia.

"You have to keep moving," he said urgently. "You have to generate some body heat." He dragged her to her feet and pushed her along. She managed to travel a few yards before tumbling into the snow again.

"Get up, Lily," he urged. "Come on."

"Oh, Eddie, I can hardly move . . ."

In the still of the forest the scraping sound of a round being chambered in a handgun was particularly noticeable. "Don't move."

Eddie looked up. A man was standing there, a Wisconsin State Trooper sergeant's badge in one hand, a 9mm in the other. "Put your hands where I can see them."

Slowly, Eddie raised his hands as did Lily. "Okay. That's good. Are either of you armed?"

"No," Eddie croaked.

"That's good." The trooper kept the gun trained on them as he pulled two sets of handcuffs from his belt. "Get on your knees and put your hands behind your backs. Understand?"

Before Eddie and Lily could reply, a gout of red blood shot out of the middle of the man's forehead, and his eyes went wide in shock. The next bullet hit him in the neck, shattering his Adam's apple and throwing him back into a snowdrift, his blood pumping out of the two killshot wounds, turning the snow crimson.

Then the helicopter passed over them. Standing in the open door was Butler, a sniper's rifle in his hands. Snow kicked up around them as Butler squeezed off a couple of shots in their direction.

For a moment, Lily forgot the cold and found the strength to run.

CHAPTER NINETEEN

As they ran they heard the engine note of the helicopter change, and it dropped from the sky, setting down somewhere further in, deeper in the forest. The chopper shut down, and the wood was quiet once again.

"They're going to track us," said Eddie, looking back at the long ragged trail of their footprints in the snow. He looked around. About six yards away was a balsam fir, the boughs heavy with snow, but beneath it was a clear circle free of snow. "This might work . . ."

They blundered through the snow to the carpet of pine needles beneath the tree, which they burrowed under. Eddie reached up to shake the branches vigorously, dumping snow on them and covering the tracks they had made getting to the safety of the tree. They lay still, scarcely daring to breathe.

"Hey, Butler," yelled one of the crewmen from the helicopter. "We got tracks over here."

"Where?" Butler shouted.

"Over here."

Eddie counted three separate voices, and all three were close now. "They only go up to here."

There was a long silence, while the three men tried to work out what happened. "They must have doubled back on their tracks," said Butler finally. "Come on, we're wasting time." Gradually the heavy footsteps receded.

Lily and Eddie rolled out of their hiding place. "Okay, we have to find some shelter."

They found it in the shape of a summer home overlooking the lake. It was shut up tight, and as they peered through the window they could see that the furniture had been covered with dust sheets.

Eddie did not hesitate to break into the cabin. With espionage and murder on his rap sheet, a little breaking and entering would hardly raise an eyebrow. Lily's lips were blue, and her eyes were glazed.

As soon as they got into the house, Eddie turned on all four burners on the old-fashioned gas stove, along with the oven, but the heat generated wasn't nearly enough to thaw out Lily.

"Stay here," he said. Eddie ran down the stairs of the house to the basement and fired up the pilot light on the hot water heater and even got the furnace to kick over. He noticed that part of the basement was a subterranean garage. A pickup truck sat there mounted on blocks. He didn't have time to examine it just then, but it looked to be in pretty good shape.

Quickly he raced back upstairs and turned on the water in the bathtub. Hot water poured into the old tub and steam rose. Eddie started to peel off his own wet clothes.

"Take off your clothes," Eddie ordered. "And get in the tub."

Lily was too tired and too cold to wonder if this was a line or if he had lost his mind. She put her trembling fingers to the zip of the parka, but she couldn't feel it. "My . . . my hands are numb . . ." A panicky looked crossed her face as it dawned on her that she could be in serious trouble. Eddie was already down to his underwear. He stepped forward and unzipped the jacket and unbuttoned her sweater, blouse, and the top button and zipper of her blue jeans. She watched him do it, grateful to him and frightened at the same time.

"Just get under the water, let the water warm you up." They both got into the steaming water, the level rising to their necks, their limbs intertwined beneath the surface. Neither spoke for a long time, they just soaked, eyes closed, absorbing the life-giving heat.

When Eddie opened his eyes fifteen or twenty minutes later, he found that she had color in her lips and her cheeks were beginning to show signs of pink. "So," she asked, a dreamy look in her eyes, "does this work with all the girls? The old, take-a-bath-with-me-in-a-house-I-broke-into trick?"

"Never fails," said Eddie. "But only with the girls I get to pull out of a creek while being chased by the police."

Lily laughed and sank a little deeper into the hot water, luxuriating in the sensation of being warm once again. "Tell me, Eddie, did you ever hear Bucky's lecture on evolution?"

Eddie shook his head. "No," he said, looking a little puzzled. "I thought I caught them all at one time or another . . . I didn't know he lectured on evolution. Evolution wasn't his field."

"Come on, Eddie," Lily said with a little giggle.

"I expected better of you. *Everything* was Bucky's field, and it wasn't a formal lecture. He started talking about it one night . . . I was a graduate research fellow at the Max Planck Institute in Germany, and Bucky was a friend of the proctor's. There was a reception for him, you know, sherry with the dean, all the bright students hobnobbing with the faculty—give them a little glory so they'll work even harder in your lab the next day . . ."

"That's how it works?"

Lily nodded, her chin making little ripples in the hot water. "Somehow the subject of evolution came up and Bucky started to speak, in German—his German was a thing of beauty, real old-fashioned Alt Deutsch—and the next thing you know, everyone in the room is listening to him. He was lecturing, but he wasn't talking down. He took evolution and turned it one hundred eighty degrees, looked at it from a different angle, and then applied it to science . . ."

Eddie was a little afraid that her flirtation with hypothermia had left her slightly unhinged, but her voice was clear and her eyes were steady.

"Bucky said that we had been taught that evolution was a nice orderly process, as regular as a railroad timetable, he said. The fish crawls onto the beach, the fish grows legs and becomes a lizard. The lizard becomes a bird, then a furry little mammal. The furry little mammal one day gets up on its hind legs and wanders around for twenty million years, during which time it works on its brain stem and opposable thumbs and then, abracadabra, becomes man . . ."

Eddie could remember that very illustration from a book he had owned when he was ten years old—*Isn't Science Wonderful?* it was called. He wondered what her point was, what she was going on about. He had no idea where this was leading, but he was sure she had a good reason to have brought it up in the first place.

"Go on," he said.

"Well," Lily said, continuing, "Bucky maintained that was not true. When dinosaurs ruled the earth, mammals were nothing more than little gray ratlike creatures living in cracks in the rocks feeding on whatever the big boys left behind. But then a huge meteorite hits the earth. The dinosaurs are out in the open, the furry gray rat mammals are stuck in the rocks. The dinosaurs are wiped out, and the rat creatures come out of the holes and they rule.

"Bucky maintained that evolution was not that nice, neat, orderly railway schedule. Rather, he said, evolution took these huge chaotic jumps, born out of chaotic, turbulent events—something unexpected, something unforeseen, something that turned over the apple cart, like a huge meteorite. And what Bucky did the other night, that was one of those jumps."

"The meteor struck," whispered Eddie. "And the dinosaurs just might not get to run the show anymore . . . and they're pissed about it."

Lily nodded. It made perfect sense. Eddie looked at her with amazement and admiration in his eyes. She had seen right through to the heart of the problem.

"Who do you figure are the dinosaurs, Lily?"

"I don't know," she said softly. "But I think we better find out . . . Or the meteorite is going to land on us."

"We have to go to Shannon," said Eddie. "We have to get to Washington. And soon."

"But how? They'll be watching the airports and the trains. And we don't have a car."

"There's a truck downstairs," said Eddie. "I can get it running. Then all we need is a little luck . . ."

Collier was plainly angry, and Shannon was loving every minute of it. They sat across from each other in a conference room in the Weather Mountain facility. Neither man knew if it was day or night.

"So you're telling me that your lapdog killed a Wisconsin State Trooper?" said Shannon.

Collier waved the question away. "I don't want to talk about it," he growled. There would be plenty of time to take care of Butler and his screwups when this particular problem had been contained. "Tell me more about Eddie Kasalivich. What kind of guy is he?"

"Don't underestimate him," said Shannon.

"Is he smart enough to keep the Bureau out of his hair?"

"He seems to be smart enough to keep you out of his hair," said Shannon. "It was a bad stroke of luck for you . . . If it had been anyone else but Eddie you wouldn't be having these headaches. All the rest were just a bunch of scientists. They could work out a sixteen-part polynomial in the time it takes to sneeze, but they couldn't operate a revolving door."

"The kid's a scrappy little bastard," Collier admitted grudgingly. "I'll give him that." Then he started to laugh, shaking his head ruefully. "Butler's seen time in six major theaters of operation. And he's getting his butt kicked all over the midwest. If he doesn't catch him, I'm gonna personally shoot him in the head."

"Butler or Kasalivich?" Shannon asked.

Collier thought for a moment, then shrugged. "One or the other," he said. "Who cares which?"

The midnight oil was also burning at Ford's command center in the Hoover Building; the difference was that the Feds knew it was night. Ford, Doyle, Williams, and Pena were watching as Rachel Fine threaded some three-quarter-inch tape into a player, plugging the contraption into a monitor. She advanced the tape a few frames at a time, the display on the monitor looking more like a slide show than a continuous videotape.

"These are video captures taken from a spy satellite that was over Chicago at the time of the explosion," Rachel Fine explained. She slowed the tape down to an even slower speed, barely a frame at a time. The laboratory exploded on the screen, the fireball slowly erupting into the sky.

"Boom," said Williams.

"Okay," said Fine, rewinding the tape and increasing the magnification. "Now observe this little streak here. She pointed to a dark-colored pixel leaving just before the blast. There was a larger set of pixels leaving first.

"I think that blurry thing is your fugitive," said Rachel Fine. "It's small enough to be a single person on a motorcycle."

"Then what's the other blurry thing?" Ford asked, "the one that's a little ahead of the *other* blurry thing leaving first."

"Well, that's an interesting question, isn't it?" said Fine. "It looks like there was a little more activity at the lab that night then we thought."

"And one blurry thing croaked Bucholtz and blew up the lab," said Caleb Williams.

"Yeah," said Pena. "But which blurry thing?"

"Rachel," Ford asked, "where did you get this?"

Rachel Fine shrugged. "I know a guy who knows a guy," she said. "No big deal."

"Would this fall into the admissible category?" said Ford.

Rachel Fine shook her head. "No, boss," she said with a slow smile. "Not even close."

"Damn." Ford turned to Williams and Pena. "What do you have on the phone taps?"

Pena opened the phone logs. "There are foundation offices in Chicago, Washington, Palo Alto.

We also had taps on Shannon's hotel in Chicago and his house in McLean ..."

"And when you ran them all together?" said Ford.

"There was one number that popped up a lot," Williams explained. "It's in Washington ... But you know what, boss?"

Ford rubbed his eyes wearily. "I know ... It doesn't exist."

"Damn," said Pena. "The boss is good."

"That's funny," said Doyle. "We've been getting a lot of that lately. Doesn't anyone think that's funny?"

"It's a riot," said Ford wearily. "You got a name for this guy who doesn't exist, who has a phone that doesn't exist?"

"That's the real funny part," said Williams. "We do."

CHAPTER TWENTY

Ford and Doyle sat in the government-issue Chevy on a quaint back street off Wisconsin Avenue in Georgetown. They looked through the gates of a large Colonial house on a very small plot of ground.

"You know how they sell real estate like that in Georgetown?" said Ford. "By the square inch."

Doyle snorted. "Shows how much you know," he said. "They don't sell houses like that. You inherit it."

"Oh," said Ford. He didn't take his eyes off the house. "You're right. I didn't know that."

"So what's the plan?"

"I'm going to get out of the car, walk up to the gate, and ring the bell," said Ford slowly. "How's that?"

"Not much of a plan, boss."

Ford shrugged. "Best I got, Seamus," he said, opening the door. He walked up the uneven red brick walk and pressed the bell. He waited a full two minutes before the intercom came to life.

"Yes?"

"This is Special Agent Raymond Ford, FBI," he said. "I wonder if we could have a chat?"

The answer was a chuckle that was cut off abruptly as the intercom went dead. Ford stood, facing the gate, feeling stymied and unwilling to walk back to Doyle and the dose of derision he was sure to serve up. Then the electronic lock on the outside gate clicked. Ford pushed his way in, walking the short path up to the front door of the house, pulling out his badge as he went.

Collier opened the door. He was wearing a rich dark blue Charvet silk dressing gown, black velvet slippers on his feet. There was a cup of coffee in his hands. He did not even bother to look at Ford's FBI badge.

"Good morning," Collier said, leading Ford into the house. Collier's house had been built in the late eighteenth century. In keeping with the styles and needs of the times, there was a fireplace in every room, and while there were a lot of rooms in the house they were small and low-ceilinged. Ford was a tall man and he had to fight the inclination to stoop.

"Can I offer you some coffee?" Collier asked solicitously. "I grind the beans myself."

"No, thanks."

"Special Agent Ford, how clever you are. To come here of all places. You are out of your mind coming here." He took a sip from his cup of coffee. "Are you sure you wouldn't like some?"

"I really don't want any coffee," said Ford firmly. "What I'd really like is some answers."

Collier chuckled that annoying, superior chuckle of his. "You don't get it, do you? Let me put it to you this way. Should it happen that you never walk out of this house, there is nothing anyone would be able to do."

"I have an agent out in the car," said Ford.

"And I have an agreement with the Embassy of Bahrain which is right next door. They have an armed staff of sixty."

Now Ford chuckled. "You're really serious about this, aren't you?"

"Oh yes, I am," he said. "And, for now, I've pissed a little higher up the wall than you."

He took another sip of coffee. "I need some milk." Abruptly, he turned and walked deeper into the house. Ford followed.

The kitchen was as well appointed as the rest of the house. The cabinets were made of burled satinwood, and the tiles on the walls were hand-made in Tuscany and hand-painted in New York. The blue enamel Le Cornu stove looked as if it had never been used.

"So, you want some answers," said Collier. He poured cream into his cup and filled another mug with coffee and handed it to Ford, as if he had made it his goal of the morning to get the agent to have a dose of caffeine. "Answers to what? Could you be more specific?"

"Sure," said Ford affably. "Who killed Professor Bucholz? Who blew up that damn laboratory? Is there a Chinese spy ring? And what the hell is James Shannon up to anyway?"

Collier didn't chuckle this time. He laughed out loud. "Shannon? Who knows? Maybe if the answer to one was the answer to all of your questions, it might solve all your problems. But, of course, you still have to run to earth that mechanic and the female chemist."

"That's the research project machinist and the physicist, I believe," Ford corrected gently.

"Your life is so complicated."

In spite of himself, Ford sipped the coffee. "You were right, this is really good coffee."

"I'm going to do what I can to help you," said Collier. He put his cup down on the countertop. Ford had the distinct impression that the gesture signaled the end of the interview.

Ford took another gulp of coffee and handed the cup back. "You know, I get the feeling you have been all along . . ."

"This is really simple, James," said Collier. "You go into the hearing room, you look grave but optimistic. You be respectful to the senators. Treat them the way you would the headmaster when you prepped at St. Paul's. Then you read the statement and then you get the hell out of there." Collier thought a moment. "Oh, and lose the damn cigar, would you? You're as bad as a baby with a pacifier."

Shannon did not look at all happy. He hated being condescended to by anyone, but he particularly loathed it when Collier did it. He scanned the statement, as if trying to burn the type off the paper with his eyes.

"Who wrote this?"

"Does it matter?"

"Yes, it matters," said Shannon testily. "If I'm going to be a mouthpiece I want to know who I'm speaking for. I'm being teed up to take the fall. And I don't like that at all, John."

Collier shrugged and didn't bother to deny the charge. Whenever an operation went awry someone had to take the fall. As long as he was not the scapegoat, he didn't care who was.

"Just read it, James," said Collier languidly. "Just read it."

"We don't know the source of the explosion, it's true. We don't know the source of the espionage, if indeed there was espionage. But we do know we are at risk," Shannon read from the script he had been given.

The senators sat at their dais looking like pompous figurines. Collier sat directly behind him in the spot usually reserved for the long-suffering but devoted wife when the subject was criminal malfeasance in high places. He had his eyes closed as Shannon read, but he was following the statement closely in his mind, the way avid classical music lovers will play the score of the concert in their minds as the orchestra plays.

There were no others in the room except for security people at the doors. This was a secret hearing requiring E-3 clearance or better. Luckily, Ford had it. He slipped into the seat next to Collier.

"Every idea that offers a competitive advantage for Americans is subject to theft. And that is the lesson to be drawn from this disaster. Security concerns must be paramount. We must begin to treat business secrets the way we once treated military ones. The cold war may be over, but we are still at war."

One of the senators leaned forward. "Mr. Shannon, yours are the words of a patriot," he intoned. "And I for one feel that you have presented a cogent argument in favor of . . ."

Collier was surprised to see Ford. He hoped it didn't show. Ford spoke as the senator blathered on. "So, how are you doing on cracking the Chinese spy ring for me?"

"I'm working on it," Collier whispered.

Another senator thought he deserved a little air time, even though he could derive no political benefit from it. It was really more of a game of good senator/bad senator. If one dished out praise, the other was sure to go and get all prickly and . . . well, senatorial.

"Mr. Shannon, there was loss of life and property in this explosion, and you are telling us very little about it or what you are doing to bring the perpetrators to swift justice."

Shannon looked puzzled. "Well, Senator, I have no police powers. The investigation of the crime falls to the brave and competent agents of the Federal Bureau of Investigation."

"Ah," said the senator. He had been in public life so long he had long since become impervious to embarrassment. "Then, Mr. Shannon, are you in a position to give this committee assurances that such an event will never occur again? I, for one, will not tolerate this kind of occurrence." It was as if he was bravely standing up to the vast majority of the population who wrongheadedly championed the cause of large explosions in urban areas.

Shannon took a deep breath. It was time to go out on a very thin limb. "Within this country's borders," said Shannon, "I do not believe such an event will ever occur again. But the price we pay might be our competitive edge. There are many threats to our way of life, gentlemen. And not all of them wear uniforms, carry guns, or set bombs."

Ford nodded appreciatively. "He's got a nice way with words," he said. "I like that."

Collier studiously ignored him.

Shannon got off the hill as fast as he could, driving back to his office in Adams Morgan as quickly as possible, darting through the midday traffic that clogged the D.C. streets, making the FBI follow team's job a little more difficult than usual.

He was safely ensconced back in his office a few moments later when his secretary knocked on his door. She entered, carrying a large but not overly elaborate bouquet of flowers. In the years that Miss Timms had worked for Shannon he had kept his personal life strictly personal.

Shannon looked mystified too. He took the card and read it. MUTANT GUY VS THE NEANDERTHAL MAN. James Shannon smiled.

"Miss Timms, is Mr. Haig around?"

"I believe so, Mr. Shannon." Haig was the security chief for the foundation. A Collier spy, of course, but as long as Shannon was aware of that, Haig could provide some valuable services.

"Ask him to come see me, would you?"

"Yes, Mr. Shannon."

He picked up the card and read it again and smiled. There seemed to be no end to Eddie's cleverness.

* * *

As the flower delivery man left the foundation, the FBI follow team surrounded him. Rachel Fine flashed her badge.

"Was that a delivery for the Moore Foundation?" she asked. "Mr. James Shannon?"

"Uh-huh, that's right" the delivery guy said nervously. "I didn't do anything wrong, did I?"

"No, no, you're fine," said Agent Wu. "What did the card say?"

"I don't know. I don't read the cards. Maybe back at the store . . ."

The owner of the florist's shop was as surprised as his driver was, but he was not in the habit of arguing with five federal agents. "The card? We throw the copies away once the delivery goes out." He bent and picked up a trash can, upending it on his counter. He rooted around in the debris and came up with a soiled piece of paper. "This is it."

Rachel Fine read it and passed it around to her colleagues. "Mutant Guy versus the Neanderthal Man . . ."

"Who placed this order?" Williams asked the owner. "Remember what they looked like?"

"It was a prepaid phone-in from Interflora," said the florist. "That comes from their central office in Indianapolis. But the order could have been made anywhere. Just about anywhere in he world . . ."

"Mutant Guy versus the Neanderthal Man," said Pena. "What could that mean? Pro wrestling match . . . Maybe a bad movie. Video store, maybe? But it means something to Shannon.

"Well, I'll bet the boss has us check on both of 'em," said Rachel Fine. "And more."

Shannon left the office in the middle of the day, got in his car, and drove to a vast shopping center in Arlington, just over the border in Virginia. The pursuit team was on him every step of the way. He parked the Jaguar up close to the doors of a supermarket and strolled in.

"Christ," said Williams. "That place is fuckin' huge. We're all going in. And I don't like that."

It had been years since Shannon had been in a supermarket, and it was sort of interesting to wander down the aisles dropping items at random into the shopping cart. He would like to have stayed a little while longer, but he had a meeting to get to. He wheeled his cart straight to the back of the giant market and leaned over the meat counter.

"I'm making a Flemish spiral roast," he told the bloodied guy behind the counter. "It's a kind of a special cut. Maybe I can talk to the butcher."

"I am the butcher, what did you want?" He looked puzzled. "What was it called again?"

"A Flemish spiral roast."

The butcher turned and surveyed the acre or so of animal parts stored in his domain.

"Never heard of it." He turned back to Shannon. "Gimme a hint . . ." But Shannon was gone, through the butcher shop, through the cold room, across the loading dock, and into the waiting van, Mr. Haig at the wheel.

"And they thought I hadn't spotted the tail," Shannon scoffed. "Amateurs . . ." As they zoomed down the highway, he flipped open a cell phone and punched in a number.

"Collier?" he said. "Where's your lapdog? I need him . . ."

CHAPTER TWENTY-ONE

The drive from Wisconsin to Washington had been a long and tedious one—just the kind of journey Lily and Eddie had been hoping for. They had driven straight through, stopping only once—in York, Pennsylvania, to wire flowers to Shannon. They arrived in Washington early in the morning, stashed the truck in a parking garage, and walked the Mall until they could get into the Smithsonian Museum.

They toured the enormous museum looking like any other pair of out-of-towners—newly-weds maybe—on a trip to take in the sights of the nation's capital. It is possible to spend an entire day in the Smithsonian, and no one noticed that they circled back every so often, revisiting the display of Neanderthal Man in the Hall of Mankind. On their sixth pass they found Shannon standing in front of the exhibit, calm and unruffled, sure that Eddie and Lily would show up eventually.

"Okay," said Eddie. "No bullshit. What's going on?"

Shannon gestured. "Come on," he said. "I want to show you something in one of the halls."

"We've been here for seven hours, Shannon," said Eddie. "Whatever it is, we've seen it already."

"Then you missed the significance of it. Come on . . ." They had no alternative but to follow him as he led them back to the vast domed rotunda, the central hub of the museum. Shannon pointed to the inscription in the drum of the dome.

"See what it says up there?" said Shannon. "See it?"

"It says Science *and* Industry. Not just science. Both entwined. If there's no practical application, then there's no point . . . That's the way the world works. Bucky wanted to give it away . . .

and then what would have happened?"

"Bucky thought that peace would break out," said Eddie, with a crooked smile. "That sounds pretty practical."

"Oh yeah," said Shannon sarcastically. "That's really practical." He tapped his temple. "Think about it, Eddie. If Bucky's experiment had suddenly been dumped on an unsuspecting world the oil companies would have gone bankrupt, the public utilities would have gone bankrupt. Whole industries would have been demolished overnight. Tens of millions would have been thrown out of work." Shannon looked at the two young people with pity in his eyes. How could they not understand the consequences of this discovery?

"Go to the Middle East. Tell the Saudis, the Iraqis, the Libyans, the Iranians, go tell them that all that oil is worthless. Think they would take that lying down? They would think that the West had screwed them once again and this time they had nothing to lose. There would have been a war, Eddie . . . And as sure as we're standing here now it would have gone nuclear."

"No," said Eddie. "It's the meteorite. It's hit, and the dinosaurs are running scared." Then his voice changed. And he sounded suddenly and profoundly sad. "And you're one of the dino-saurs, Shannon. Lily was right, you're one of them. Maybe you didn't kill Bucky, but you think it had to be done. You probably thought it was extreme but expedient or some other nice, neat, clean phrase."

"My God," said Lily. "And Bucky trusted you. He considered you a friend of his."

"He considered me a source of funds," said Shannon bitterly. He decided that he had had his fill of debate and ethereal talk. "I'm not going to coddle you anymore, Eddie. The job needs to be finished. The experiment needs to be verified. You need to go back to work, Eddie."

"I don't think so." Eddie's voice was loud in the quiet space.

Shannon gestured to him to keep it down. "You don't have a choice, Eddie. They will do what they have to do."

"Then why frame me? Why me?"

"They thought you were just some convenient gearhead putz they could hang this on. You weren't supposed to see Bucky dead. If you hadn't seen him, none of this would have hap-pened. Lily was just part of the package. It made it seem more real, that's all."

"This is crazy," said Eddie, staring at the floor.

"Grow up Eddie. Science and industry. Science *and* industry. That's the way the world works."

The muscles in Eddie's jaw flexed, as if he was forcing himself not to speak. But he was not going to give an inch.

"Eddie," said Shannon. "It doesn't have to be this way. You can still be part of the experiment."

"The world works the way we make it work," Eddie said finally. "Everything else is bullshit you say to make yourself feel better about the shitty things you do to get what you want."

Shannon sighed. "Okay . . ." He nodded at someone beyond Eddie's line of sight, and Butler and his merry band stepped out from behind a display case.

Three of the men walked toward Lily and Eddie, one reaching for Eddie, the other for Lily; the third was backup. The thug going for Eddie figured to take him easily. A mistake. Eddie sidestepped the man, grabbed him by the shoulders and threw him through the glass of the Neanderthal exhibit. He tumbled, his hands and face lacerated. Lily grabbed the Neanderthal's sling and rock and smashed her attacker square in the face.

Then they ran.

Butler had expected this to be a pretty easy takedown, but he had taken the precaution of posting men all over the museum. The instant things started to go wrong, he had his radio out and was alerting all of his goons, moving them around the gigantic museum like pieces on a chessboard.

The Smithsonian security guards had heard the smashing glass and the shouts and cries of the injured and had alerted the parks service police.

The frantic calls for police assistance at the Smithsonian Institution chattered out of the scanners in the FBI building.

"Hey," said Doyle. "Listen to that . . . Sounds like a heist at the Smithsonian Museum."

"Don't touch that scanner," Ford ordered. "Guess who lives at the Smithsonian, Seamus?"

"The Neanderthal Man?"

Lily and Eddie raced down a corridor on the second floor, pounding down the marble floor as fast as they could, racing into the two-story Hall of Transportation. The vast upper level of the room was filled with a variety of old steam locomotives, a New York streetcar from the turn of the century, and a number of old airplanes. The atrium of the room was dominated by a life-sized working model of an old Boeing seven-twenty-seven that flew above the Smithsonian collection of vintage American and European automobiles displayed on the floor below.

There were three thugs ahead of Lily and Eddie and three behind. They were trapped in the hall.

"Come on," said Eddie. He climbed up onto the parapet of the atrium and pulled her after him. Then, together, they leaped off the rail and on to the wing of the seven-twenty-seven, the display rocking sickeningly as it took their weight. Lily dove through the wing hatch into the dusty interior of the plane.

The avionics well was open and without thinking, Lily jumped into it, dropping into the dark underbelly of the aircraft. The gloom and the dust were suffocating. All she could do was crawl on her stomach towards a shaft of light in the middle of the fuselage. She had no idea where Eddie was. Reaching the light, she could see that she was situated just above the under-carriage of the aircraft, the long hydraulic stems and the fat tires dangling from the underside.

She shimmied down to the tire and hung there

for a moment, looking down. She had no idea how far she was about to fall, but she knew there was no going back. Taking a deep breath she let go and dropped.

A split second later she found herself sprawled flat on her back in the commodious rear seat of a 1909 Simplex touring car. Lily scrambled out of it, darted under the rope surrounding it, and tried to join a group of tourists who were being cleared from the hall by harried security guards.

The tourists seemed annoyed at being moved along before closing time. "But we just got here!" protested a man with twin cameras looped across his chest like bandoleers.

"I'm sorry," said one of the guards. "I'm sorry. But we have been given orders to close the museum immediately."

Lily joined the crowd being ushered toward one of the emergency exits. She did her best to look annoyed and disappointed. As she drew nearer to the way out, she felt a little bubble of elation. She was going to make it—then a woman sidled up next to her, gave her a friendly smile, and waved a small glass vial under her nose. The vapors went straight to her brain and she passed out, as if someone had thrown a switch.

Eddie had raced across one wing of the seven-twenty-seven, clambered over the main fuselage to the other wing, using the old plane as a bridge spanning from one side of the atrium to the other. He found a set of service stairs and charged down them, emerging in another swarm of museum-goers who were being herded toward the exit. He was outside just in time to see Butler and the female operative loading Lilly into a van, the vehicle racing away from the curb before the doors were even closed. Eddie chased after it, but there was no way he was going to catch it. He stopped in the middle of the street and strained to see the license plate.

"Three-six-five-MJ-two," he chanted. "Three-six-five-MJ-two." Then it was gone and he was alone.

Shannon was still in the rotunda, listening to the alarm and tumult echoing all over the venerable museum, when Ford and his men came down the steps from the upper floors of the building. Eddie was a young fool, but he found he could not quite suppress a sneaking admiration for him. The FBI, the CIA, the weight of the American government—he didn't seem to care how powerful the forces were that were arrayed against him. He would take anyone on.

"Well, well, well," said Ford. "If it isn't our friend Mr. Shannon ... Visiting the Neanderthal Man by any chance?" He stopped and stood right in front of Shannon. "Okay," he said. "Where did he go?"

"Neanderthal Man?" said Shannon innocently. "The original is still here, I think. Though reasonable facsimiles abound." Then he started for the door. But Ford blocked his path.

Shannon was not impressed. "Are you arresting me, Agent Ford? Because if you are not, you are in my way."

"No," said Ford with a quick shake of his head. "But I made a deal. If I don't get Eddie, I get you."

"Oh, I don't think that's too likely . . ."

"Money and influence," said Ford. "You think that's going to protect you forever."

"Gosh," said Shannon. "I'd be really surprised if it didn't. Money and influence protects better than any firearm. The people with money and influence tell the people with guns who to shoot."

"Not when the influence runs out or when the money runs dry," said Ford. "Not when you become a liability." He shrugged. "You or Eddie.

I get one or the other and I'm happy. Though I'm sort of getting to like Eddie."

"That happens the more you get to know him," said Shannon. "He grows on you."

"So, if I had a choice, I'd take you."

"Oh well," said Shannon. "Everybody wants what they can't have. You should set more realistic goals for yourself, Agent Ford. I have a feeling if you did, your life would be so much happier . . ."

CHAPTER TWENTY-
TWO

Eddie walked down Independence Avenue, his head down, his shoulders hunched, passing the Capitol and the attendant buildings. He was fighting a case of rising paranoia. There seemed to be cops at every intersection, and he winced every time a helicopter passed over head.

The streets behind the Capitol building were poor and thronged with downcast men like himself. He stood for a moment on a corner wondering what to do next . . . He could not think of a thing. For once he was fresh out of ideas. Yet another police car was cruising down the block and Eddie, as casually as he could, turned his back and ambled down a side street.

A homeless man, a collection of dirty rags and thin limbs, sat on a heating grate in front of a church, watching him as he passed.

"Hey mister," he shouted. "Spare some change? A quarter? What's a quarter? Nothin'."

Eddie, trapped in his own problems, ignored him, walking by without a glance in his direction.

"Hey!" the homeless man shouted after him. "What am I? Invisible? You didn't even see me! You son of a bitch!"

Eddie stopped dead in his tracks, thought a moment, then turned and walked back to the man. The homeless, so prevalent on the streets of American cities, had become invisible. People had become so used to the sight of poverty and suffering they just didn't see it anymore.

Eddie looked down at the homeless man. "You're right . . . You are invisible," he said.

The man looked offended. He rearranged his rags, as if gathering up what remained of his pride and looked away, gazing down the street.

"Why you fucking with me? I didn't do nothin' to you."

"Can I share your grate?" Eddie asked. "I'm cold too. I'll give you twenty bucks."

The man thought about it for a moment. It was a pretty bizarre request, but twenty bucks was twenty bucks . . . He slid over a little, making room for him. Eddie sat down and offered his hand.

"Eddie."

"Joe," he said as they shook hands.

Eddie looked up the street. So, he thought, this was the view from rock bottom. A police car rolled by and he tensed, but the cops didn't even bother to slow down. For the first time in hours, Eddie could relax for a moment.

"Hey, Eddie . . ."

"Yeah, Joe."

"Was you ever in the armed forces?"

"No," Eddie replied. "No, never. You?"

"I was," said Joe. "That was where my own problems started. I think it was the stuff they sprayed in the Gulf . . ." He tapped his head and lowered his voice. "I hear people talking to me. In my head. People who aren't there. They're talking to me, but they ain't here. What about you?"

"The CIA's trying to kill me. They blew up the place where I used to work and kidnapped this girl I know . . . Oh yeah, I'm the subject of a nationwide manhunt, and the FBI wants to frame me . . ."

Joe nodded. "You too? I know a couple of people with problems like yours. You know Louis? He's a fella hangs around K Street Northeast. He was telling me the other day that he has really terrible problems with the CIA boys. They just won't leave that poor man alone . . ."

Across the street, a line was forming up in front of the parish house of the church, a ragged queue of homeless men, some of them shouting and pushing, desperate to get into the soup kitchen.

"Some people have no manners," said Joe, watching as the crowd grew more unruly. An elderly priest and a couple of harried volunteers were not up to the task of keeping order.

Joe leaned over close to Eddie. "Tell me, Eddie. The district cops . . . Are they in on it with the CIA guys?"

"They could be," said Eddie seriously. "Why do you ask?"

" 'Cause they're going to be here in a few minutes. The kitchen can only feed forty, fifty people tops. And near as three hundred show most nights." Joe glanced over at the growing crowd. "They come about twice a week to break up this mess. They crack a couple of heads ... You know, no big deal."

Eddie thought fast. "Hey, Joe," said Eddie. "You want to make a quick fifty bucks?"

Joe did not hesitate. "Yep."

"When the cops get here, keep them busy for a couple of minutes." Eddie slipped him two twenties and a ten.

"Am I going to jail?" Joe asked.

"Maybe."

Joe shrugged. "Who cares? It's warm. They feed you."

"Thanks, man."

Joe was absolutely correct. As the crowd grew larger, filling the sidewalk and spilling into the street, the disorderly element grew larger too. Pushing and shoving in the line, fistfights breaking out. Sure enough, a police cruiser pulled up, the siren whooping. The two cops got out of their car, slapping their billies in their hands.

"Okay," roared one of the cops. "Let's back it up here, let's get out of the street. Let's get outta the street. On the sidewalk."

"Trouble ain't here, officer," said one of the

homeless men. "The bad boys pushed their way inside, making trouble for the priest."

As the two cops waded through the crowd, Eddie emerged from the shadows and slid into the police cruiser. Mounted between the two front bucket seats of the police car was a glowing green screen of the onboard computer, wired into the national police ID net.

Eddie glanced over his shoulder and saw that the crowd inside the mission was growing. He could hear Joe's voice, bellowing about police racism and the general mistreatment of combat veterans.

He chose LICENSE CHECK from a menu, typed in the state, asked for wanteds, warrants, and addresses and then slotted in the tag number.

"Three-six-five-MJ-two." He hit the enter key hard. The screen went blank except for the prompt: TRANSMITTING. Fifteen seconds passed before TRANSMITTING changed to SEARCHING.

The machine clicked and blinked as it considered Eddie's request. Another thirty seconds passed.

"Come on . . .," Eddie whispered. *"Come on!"*

Joe's voice was louder now. "Under arrest! What the fuck you mean under arrest! Whad'I do, man!"

Then the address popped up on the screen. The van was registered as a commercial vehicle. "SHELBYVILLE CONSTRUCTION INC. 10888 ROUTE 12 RFD, SHELBYVILLE, VIRGINIA." He didn't have a pen and paper, so he yanked one out of the cop's citation books and scribbled the address on his arm. And where the hell was Shelbyville? There was a thick book of maps on the dash. He grabbed it and stuffed it into his jacket and slipped out of the cruiser just as the two cops hauled Joe out of the soup kitchen, his hands cuffed behind his back.

Lily could not move and through her fogged brain she had the very distinct sensation of a long and precipitous fall. Suddenly, there was light in one of her eyes.

"She's waking up." The voice was vaguely familiar. She knew she had heard it before, but in her befuddled state she could not place it.

"Don't do that, Butler . . ." She knew that voice too, but this one was more familiar than the other. "Lily, Lily . . ."

Her eyes fluttered open, and she found that she was looking into the eyes of James Shannon.

"Hi," he said. "I'm sorry it had to be this way."

She was awake enough to realize that she had been strapped to a wheelchair and that the falling sensation came from the fact that she was in a vast, round elevator. She was also awake enough to hate him.

The elevator slowed, then stopped, the doors sweeping open silently. Butler pushed the chair into the stone passageway. She looked at the hewn walls and realized that she was deep underground, and that could only mean one thing. Somewhere in the back of her mind she remembered reading about an extensive underground complex that had been constructed for a single, gigantic project.

"This is a weapons facility," she said.

"No," said Shannon in mock surprise. "That's very clever of you, Lily."

"Congress defunded the Critical Path project."

Shannon nodded. "That's true." He shrugged. "They made a mistake. We corrected it. Butler, unstrap her."

"I'd rather not," said Butler.

"I don't care what you'd rather."

Butler frowned but did what he was told. Lily stood up, but she was still unsteady on her feet from the effects of the drug. Shannon took her by the arm and walked her down the wide corridor and into the large conference room.

Collier was seated at his console buying and selling some commodity on the other side of the world. He made a couple of hundred thousand dollars in artichoke futures and turned away from his screens.

"Why don't you sit down, Lily?"

Lily did not want to take anything from them, not even anything as insignificant as a seat, but she still felt woozy. Collier pushed a carafe of water and a glass across the table.

"Water," he said. "You have to drink plenty of water. That stuff they drugged you with, it's very astringent. Plus the air is so dry down here. Now, Lily. Truthfully we were hoping to obtain the services of your friend Eddie Kasalivich, but given his absence we'd like to offer you the opportunity to continue the work you started with Dr. Bucholtz. We would like you to head the project in his place."

It took a moment to for her to comprehend the sheer gall of the offer. "You're serious."

"Oh yes," said Collier. "Quite serious. We've been following your work for a long time. We're very impressed."

Lily laughed. "I'm supposed to be flattered? Do you drug and kidnap everyone whose work impresses you so much?"

"No," said Collier. "Not everyone."

"Where's Dr. Chen?"

"Chen. Ahhh . . . When we couldn't get it to work, we asked him what we were doing wrong. Unfortunately we ended up asking him very vigorously."

"You mean you killed him."

Behind her, Butler smirked a little bit.

"Nobody wanted it that way," said Collier, as if there had been a minor breech of etiquette. "We thought he was being inscrutable. It turns out he just didn't know the answers to our questions." Collier flicked on his computer screens again. "Mr. Shannon will give you the tour . . ."

Shannon led her through the busy passageways of the underground complex, directing her to a set of heavy steel doors that parted silently when Shannon punched a number into the encrypted keypad set in the rock. They stepped into a vast oval room, the ceiling curving gently.

Lily could not suppress a gasp of surprise. Standing in the middle of the enormous space was an exact replica of the Bessemer Project rig, reproduced down to its smallest detail. There were racks and racks of equipment, cases of tools, boxes of raw materials. There was even a stereo with a collection of tapes and CDs. She studied the apparatus for a moment or two, then turned on Shannon. She was all business now.

"So what happens if I can't get it to work? Do you question me vigorously as you did to Chen?"

Shannon thought it over. "If you're working in good faith and can't achieve a successful conclusion to the experiment . . ." He let her hang for a moment, enjoying the tease. "Hmmmm, I guess we'll have to see what happens when we get there. Won't we, Lily?"

"You are a pathetic little freak," she sneered. "How's this for some good faith advice: this thing will never work. Not even if Eddie was here. Any damn fool could see it at a glance."

"Really? Why is that?"

"The reaction is trigger by a laser," said Lily. "Without ten kilojoules you can't get this thing to start."

"Oh," said Shannon, leading her to a door on the far side of the room. "We thought of that detail." He entered his number in another keypad. "We have a color-tuned ten *mega*joule implementation."

"That's impossible! There was only one of those ever built . . ." Suddenly she knew what he was going to say next.

The doors slid into the walls, and they stepped into the laser room. It was four stories high, so towering that light did not reach all the way to the ceiling. The laser stood in the middle of the room, flanked by a complicated series of computer-controlled front-surface mirrors that would direct the beam along a variety of paths, including one straight into the lab and the mechanism.

"That's right, Lily. There's only one. Built for SDI. Star Wars they called it in the press. It was going to kill satellites. Now it's mine."

Butler walked into the room, looking Lily over in a way that made her flesh crawl. She couldn't tell if he had sex or violence on his mind . . . probably both.

"There's one more thing I want you to see . . ." Shannon led her to a dim corner of the laser room. A lockdown cage had been built against the walls. Once intended for the storage of fragile equipment, precious metals, and the like, Lily could see that it had been converted into a bedroom . . . or rather, a cell. There was a cot, a desk, a lamp, and a camp toilet.

"My apologies," said Shannon. He really did sound sorry about the crudity of the accommodations. "This is our facility for visiting scientists that we're not quite sure are cooperative yet. The regular living quarters are quite a bit nicer."

"You're not putting me in there."

"No. I'm not. Mr. Butler is."

Butler shoved her into the cage and locked the door.

"Now Lily, if you need anything," said Shannon solicitously, "anything at all . . . that's just too damn bad."

The two men walked away, both of them laughing at Shannon's little joke. She listened to their laughter and the click of their heels as they receded until the sounds faded away completely and she was left alone in oppressive silence.

From time to time Ford's team of agents was permitted to go home, have a life, have a meal with their families, even a night of uninterrupted sleep. This was one such night.

Such luxuries did not apply to Doyle and Ford. They were both tired as hell, but they had resigned from normal life years before. Doyle set a Styrofoam cup of coffee down in front of Ford. The boss pushed it away.

"Why don't you just bring me the coffee beans?" said Ford. "I'll just chew them instead."

"I poured the hot water through the beans you chewed to make this coffee. That's all you get."

Ford picked up the cup, sipped, and made a face. "I don't like any of this," he said unhappily.

"There's tea," said Doyle.

"That's not what I meant, and you know it."

"You read me like a book, boss."

"If Eddie did it, why did he meet Shannon in a public place?" He answered his own question. "Why? Because he didn't trust Shannon. If the kid is dirty, and they're all dirty, why doesn't he go somewhere that doesn't exist?"

"Or did he do that already and that's why we can't find him," said Doyle.

"We haven't been able to find him all along," said Ford. He took his wallet out of his suit coat pocket, counted out five crinkled twenties and placed them on the desk in front of him. "A hundred bucks says Eddie didn't do it."

"Well, if he didn't do it," said Doyle, "then you become the guy who ordered a nationwide manhunt for an innocent party."

Both men knew that would not set well with the FBI nor do anything to enhance Ford's reputation. But somehow he didn't give a damn about that. "Look, Seamus, let's just make sure we don't shoot him."

CHAPTER TWENTY-
THREE

Eddie paid the parking bill, retrieved the stolen pickup from the garage, and drove through the deserted early morning streets of Washington D.C. He had studied the police maps closely, and so got on the famous Washington Beltway at Falls Church, then switched to the equally famous (but for more picturesque reasons) Route 66, which would lead him into the heart of rural Virginia.

He stashed the pickup truck by the side of the road, a mile or so from the construction site, and made his way overland. It was huge. There were piles of gravel half an acre large, dozens of giant pieces of earth-moving machinery, and an ugly scar cut into the side of Weather Mountain, a black hole drilled down into the rock like a mineshaft. But it was only when he spotted the elaborate security did he realize that he was on the right track. Only very secret projects had electrified fences, guard gates, and roving security patrols.

There was no obvious way in, and for a moment he despaired. Then he heard the low rumbling, and the first of a long line of flatbed trucks heavily laden with construction equipment and material came rolling down the road. The cabs were crammed with workers, the day shift moving in to take over the job from the weary night shift.

The trucks rumbled down the dirt access road, the engines groaning as the drivers slowed and downshifted at the bottom of a long grade, the transmissions grumbling in complaint at such harsh treatment. The last truck in the line was carrying a pyramid of concrete culvert pipes. It was Eddie's only chance. He broke from his cover, reached the pipe truck as it slowed, grabbed the back and hauled himself up onto the bed and into the dark recesses of the pipe.

The guards on the gate were so used to this morning convoy, they just waved the trucks through.

Once inside the compound, Eddie slipped out of his hiding place and from there on in, just followed the crowd. The workers were streaming into a prefab shed set on one corner of the site, Eddie hanging back a bit until he made sure this wasn't some kind of shape up or roll call, some little check in procedure that would bring him face-to-face with officials.

Suddenly he felt a very heavy hand on his shoulder, and he damned near jumped out of his skin. He had been accosted by a square-shaped, refrigerator-sized man dressed in a plaid shirt and beat-up blue jeans.

"Forget something?"

Eddie felt a surge of panic. "Ahhh . . ."

The big man smiled and waved an aluminum lunch box in his face. "You leave your chow on the truck? You know the rule: once you're in the hole, you can't leave till the shift change. I dunno about you, but I get kinda hungry down there."

Eddie realized that almost everyone was toting a lunch pail. He clutched his stomach. "Oh man, are you kidding? I was so drunk last night

. . . I even think about food, I'll puke enough to fill that goddamned hole!''

The huge guy guffawed. ''Jeez, that's a lotta puke. But I hear ya. Been there myself a couple of times . . .''

The shed was a changing room, with hundreds of pairs of identical overalls dangling from the ceiling, rows of denims on pulleys. Workers were hauling them down at random, so Eddie grabbed the nearest rope and yanked a set down. Once he had the overalls on along with a yellow hardhat, a miner's lamp on the brim, he looked like everyone else on the project, just another one of the drones of the world that people like Shannon held in such contempt.

Off the changing room was one of the site offices, a couple of dented gray metal desks covered with plans and diagrams. The room was empty. A phone rang monotonously. Walking as if he knew exactly what he was doing, Eddie strode into the cramped room and picked up the phone with one hand while pressing down on the disconnect button with the other. He shifted the phone to the crook of his shoulder and leaned over the plans spread out in front of him, nodding from time to time, like a dutiful worker taking orders from a foreman.

Eddie had been poring over blueprints since first discovering these magical documents when he was ten years old. But these made no sense.

"Two miles long," he said, as if speaking into the phone. "Case-hardened walls, three hundred feet below the surface . . . but it goes nowhere." Eddie stared hard. "What are you doing here, Shannon? What is it that you don't want anyone to see?" He flipped through the stack of plans.

"Where did you put her?" he mumbled. On one of the plans there was a tiny clue. A drainage tunnel coming off the tube was marked as running from Main Lab to Pumping Room B. Eddie looked around quickly and then tore the page from the binder, quickly stuffing it into his overall pockets.

Eddie made his way into the main tunnel, where numbers spray-painted on the walls corresponded to the numbers on his stolen blueprints. The deeper he went into the tunnel the louder the sound of a generator or an engine became.

Pumping Room B was right where the blueprints said it would be. There was a plating layer of rebar against the wall, some unfinished casing, and the drainage hole itself. Hundreds of gallons of water a second gushed out of the opening, propelled by the temporary pump that hacked away ceaselessly. The water poured through a yellow plastic catch net and into a discharge pipe that ran down the tunnel.

Eddie looked at the torrent, swallowed hard, climbed the rebars, and with the water trying to blast him out, he forced his way in. Once inside, he discovered the water filled only three-quarters of the pipe, but the current was strong and continued to try to force him out, the flow building in a wave against his chest. It was dark inside the pipe, and he fumbled for the headlight on his hardhat, the thin beam stabbing into the shadow as he battled his way against the cold, rushing water.

Butler unlocked Lily's cage and stepped aside for Shannon.

"Good morning, Lily."

"Is it?"

"I can assure you that it is morning," said Shannon. "Whether it turns out to be a good one is entirely up to you."

She had had all night to make up her mind. "You killed Bucky," she spat, hatred in her eyes.

"I am getting a little tired of that refrain, Lily. God knows I've heard it enough by now." Behind him Butler scoffed at the suggestion that Shannon had killed the professor. As if James Shannon had the balls to do the job.

"Actually, though, I did not kill Bucky."

"Was it your toy monkey here who did the job?"

"He's not my toy monkey," said Shannon irritably. "But in point of fact, I believe he did. You might remember that, because Mr. Butler will be accompanying you today. Just to make sure you don't do anything stupid."

Butler sat in a straightback chair, tilting it back on its rear legs, watching Lily's every move as she wandered around the experiment. She circled it warily as if it was a sleeping wild beast that could awaken at any moment. The workbenches were stocked with everything the Chicago lab had possessed and then some. There was even a Mutant Guy action figure perched on the desk that Chen would have occupied . . . She didn't know what the hell to do, beyond knowing that she had to escape. But how, she had no idea.

There was a whirring from the high-tech lock on the door, and the panels divided. A blond young man entered, pushing a computer on a

stand entered. Lily stared at him for a moment.
"I know you . . ."

"Yeah, we overlapped on the Chicago project
for a few weeks. You were just coming as I was
leaving. Jake Lucas," he said, holding out his
hand.

Lily took it tentatively, wondering if he was a
volunteer or slave labor like herself. She remembered now. He had been a tech under Eddie's
command, but one day he called in his resigna-
tion and vanished, not even bothering to pick up
his last paycheck.

"So cool you're here, Lily," Lucas said.

"I don't get it," she said. "What are you doing?"

"I'm bringing you a computer workstation,"
said Lucas. "Shannon said you could have one
as long as there was no modem link to the outside world. But don't take it personally. None of
the scientists or techs have it. This is pretty top
secret stuff, and they can't take the risk, you
know?"

"No, no, no . . . What are you doing *here*?"

Lucas looked at her as if the answer was obvious. "I'm working on the project. It's great
here. The facilities are amazing. Have they
showed you the whole place? Have you seen the

laser?'' He was as enthusiastic as a kid who has been promised a new bike at Christmas time.

She still did not know if he was an ally. Maybe he was just an innocent who did not know the depth of the evil he had become involved in. "The food is really good too. No booze though. Though we all suspect that Shannon and Collier and some of the upper crust have a stash.''

"Jake," said Lily quietly. "Shannon and the rest of them killed Bucky. They stole his experiments. They destroyed the Chicago lab.''

Lucas laughed. "What are you talking about? The Chinese killed Bucky, everyone knows that. Chen sold out the whole damn project. I know he was a friend of yours, but I never trusted him. Not for a minute. And do you think I don't know about the explosion? Hey, we have cable down here. That's wild about Eddie Kasalivich, huh? Who'd have thought it? Still waters and all that shit. Still, I never thought he'd pull a stunt like that. Did you hear he murdered a state trooper up there in Wisconsin or somewhere?

Across the room, Butler laughed.

"So you bought their line," said Lily sadly.

"Come on, Lily, this is the government . . . This place is incredible. And the pay! Jesus, Shannon bought me a boat as a signing bonus.

You . . . you'll be able to get a house in Bermuda.
Ever been there? That's where I want to keep my
boat. It's beautiful down there . . . Bucky was a
dreamer, Lily. And he trusted the wrong people.
Look what happened to him."

"Bucky was a genius," Lily insisted.

Lucas snorted, "Bucky was gonna die broke,"
as if that was the worst fate a man could suffer,
proof that a life had been wasted.

CHAPTER TWENTY-FOUR

When Lucas left, Lily knew she was alone, without friends or allies there deep underground. If she were going to get out, she would have to get herself out. She returned to the workbench and looked over the array of tools, noticing in particular a large supply of shrink tubing and a heat gun. A plan was beginning to form in her mind.

She put her arms around a tank of pressurized helium and tried to lift it, but she couldn't. Avoiding eye contact with Butler, she spoke. "I need to move this tank about three feet," she said. "I can't lift it. Can you call someone for me?"

Butler's features formed themselves into a sneer. "I'll do it," he said, getting out of his chair. She shrank away from him as if he was the Antichrist, retreating a few feet, standing near a pile of heavy pipes.

Butler grabbed the tank and lifted it. Lily didn't hesitate for a second. She hefted a length of pipe and swung it with all the power she could muster. The full weight of the metal smacked hard against Butler's skull, the impact sounding like a baseball bat hitting a watermelon. Butler went down as if he had been cut off at the knees, but Lily was horrified to see that he wasn't out cold. He was stunned and not ready to fight back—not yet anyway—but he was struggling back to full consciousness.

She grabbed an entire package of shrink tubing, three feet long and thirty strands thick. Kicking Butler over on his stomach, she gathered his wrists and tethered them with one big overhand knot. It was not enough to hold a six-year-old—until she hit it with the heat gun. The plastic contracted tightly, sucking down with a vengeance and locking fast. The pressure made the blue veins in his hands bulge. His ankles got the same treatment.

The door was locked, of course. There was no keyhole, no handle, nothing she could get her hands on. The only way out was by activating the electronic keypad. Frantically, she pounded numbers at random, but there was no chance that she would hit on the exit code simply by accident.

But Lily had come that far. She refused to be overwhelmed by a setback. Picking up her iron rod she marched back to Butler and stood over him, the pipe resting on her shoulder as if she was a batter on deck.

Despite having the worst headache of his life, Butler rolled over on his back and looked up at Lily. The left side of his face was horribly bruised and swollen, and it hurt to smile, but he couldn't help himself.

"What are you going to do now, Lily?"

She raised the pipe threateningly. "Tell me the code."

"No." He laughed through broken teeth. "You're not going to beat me to death. So why don't you just get this shit off my wrists and ankles, and we can stop this charade. Don't worry. You won't get in trouble for cracking me with that thing. Shannon'll probably think it's funny. Collier will wish he did it himself. Me, though, you'd have to worry about . . . I admit that. But I follow orders until I don't have to anymore."

"Shut up," Lily snarled.

"Make me."

"Okay." She dropped the pipe and unrolled a long length of gaffer tape, wrapping it around his mouth and head. She picked up the phone and listened to the dial tone—but who would she call? Lily dropped the handset down onto the cradle. The despair was beginning to come on . . .

Just then the door beeped and slid open, and a worker ambled into the room. Butler, saw him and started to grunt behind his gag, desperate to attract his attention. Lily walked over to the man.

"Hi, I'm glad you came so fast. I was supposed to get some parallel cable but the guy never came back and—"

"Lily," said Eddie. "It's me." He rushed toward her, but she backed away, her world collapsing once again.

"Did . . . did they catch you?"

Eddie shook his head. "No."

The sadness almost crushed her, then it was replaced by disgust. There could only be one other answer. "They offered you lots of money," she said hollowly. "And all the high-tech crap you could ever want, right?"

"No," he said. "Of course not. I broke into this place to get you out of it."

She really wanted to believe that, but she had long since passed through the looking glass.

"Promise me it's true."

"What else would I be doing here? I crawled through a drainage pipe. Look at me, I'm soaking wet."

Lily threw her arms around him. He was undeniably damp. Over his shoulder, though, she saw something that made her stomach lurch. "Oh God, you let the door lock behind you. We're stuck in here."

Eddie looked across the room to the vast array of shiny new gear. "Oh Jeez," he said deadpan. "If only I had a carbide saw or a horizontal drill press or . . ." His eyes alighted on Butler, prone on the floor, the length of pipe next to him.

"Who's that?"

"He killed Bucky."

"And you hit him with that pole?"

Lily nodded. "Sometimes when things don't work, you just need to whack 'em with something."

"Words to live by."

It took about two hours for Eddie to get his ducks in a row, throwing together makeshift devices, each one necessary for their plan. He took a carbon saw to the door first so they would have their escape path in place when the time came to run. Then he seated himself at the workbench with a soldering iron and some printed circuits, jury-rigging two devices—they weren't pretty but they worked.

While Lily started the preliminary steps to operating the experiment, he seated himself at the computer and spent thirty minutes there, typing furiously, pausing to slide disks into the A drive every few minutes. Finally, they were ready . . . or as ready as they were ever going to be.

Lily powered up the laser, the whole giant room thrumming with energy as the electrical feed poured in. While she worked, Eddie attached a long coil of wire to the bookshelf stereo, then ransacked the pile of tapes and compact discs stacked next to it.

"Anywhere there are techs working all night, there's music," he announced. "Really shitty music . . . Female vocalist, Europop, Paul Simon . . ." Then he found what he was looking for. "*Sucking the Seventies*. This ought to do." He put the tape in his pocket and picked up the phone, dialing a number quickly. "Agent Ford, please—Eddie Kasalivich."

Ford was on the line in an instant. "This is Eddie. Listen, I'm in Shelbyville, Virginia. Underground. In a bunker. With all my wild, radical, bomb-making Chinese-loving buddies. You need to come here right away and arrest me and all the rest of them. You got that?"

"Got it. Radical bomb network . . . Come on, Eddie, I know you're a smart guy. Give me the same respect. You really expect me to believe that?"

"I don't care either way, Ford. Are you coming or not?"

Ford laughed. "Absolutely."

Lily was ready, the experiment was set to go on-line. Eddie stuffed the tape into the drive and hit play. He grabbed his coil of wire, running through the room to the experiment, snaking the coil into the capacitor regulators. It was a crude piece of engineering, but it was the best time-delay fuse he could arrange on the spur of the moment.

The opening chords of the song "Can't You

Hear Me Knocking" were just starting up.

"They want hydrogen?" said Eddie. "We'll give 'em hydrogen." Suddenly he was elated, almost giddy, as if the gloom and terror of the last few days had finally burned off.

The laser beam followed the path of mirrors from the room next door and hit its proper entry point on the rig. The water tanks began to roil.

"We should have six million cubic feet of hydrogen in just over twelve minutes," said Lily.

"Then we should probably leave."

The Hazardous Response Team, the FBI Swat unit based in Quantico, Virginia, came swooping down on the building site, all six choppers hitting the ground at the same time. Armed and armored agents poured out, establishing a perimeter, covering everyone and everything in sight.

The guard at the checkpoint leaped for a phone, but Ford strode over and yanked the instrument out of his hand. "I wouldn't do that, sonny."

"This is a private installation, sir," the guard said, as if he was a Marine instead of a rent-a-cop. "There is no trespassing. You can't enter here."

"That's incorrect. I am a Federal law enforcement officer. I have probable cause and I can go anywhere I damn well please. Son, do you really want to get killed for minimum wage?"

That gave the young man pause. Put that way . . .

When the laser hit peak power, the internal security computer detected a threat of fire in the underground installation and automatically triggered the alarm system. Bells rang and sirens howled. An unnaturally calm voice issued from the public address speakers.

"What the hell is that?" said Collier.

"Warning," the PA cooed. "Warning. Evacuate. Explosive atmosphere detected."

"That's bullshit!" Shannon snarled. "That clever little bitch figured some way to trigger the alarm."

He yanked a big old Army Colt .45 from Collier's desk and chambered a round. "Your boy Butler is around here somewhere with his head up his ass," Shannon said. "I'm going to finish this myself." He stuffed his cigar into his mouth and lit it.

In fact, Butler was still lying on the floor of the Bessemer Room, looking at the apparatus as it heated and trembled under the force of the power that had been unleashed on it. For once, Butler was terrified—after all, he was lying at ground zero.

Eddie peeked into the corridor beyond the lab. There was controlled pandemonium out there. People lining up for the packed elevators. No one was going to notice them out there.

"Let's go," said Eddie.

"What about him?" Lily pointed to Butler. The man was trying to scream behind his gag.

Eddie was unmoved. "He put a plastic bag over Bucky's head and watched him die. Maybe you can hop out in time to get arrested. Come on."

They were racing down the main corridor, joining the stream of people making for the emergency exits. Suddenly an arm shot out of a doorway, hitting Eddie in the neck, clotheslining him. Eddie got up, furious, but found he was looking straight into the barrel of Shannon's .45.

"How the hell did you get here, Eddie?" Shannon asked. "Never mind. We'll talk about it some other time."

"Hey," said Eddie. "You finally lit that stogie."

"Go shut this thing off," Shannon ordered.

"You are a terrible negotiator, Shannon," said Eddie coldly. "Pull the trigger. Go on."

The public address was a little more frantic now: "Explosive atmosphere. Explosive atmosphere. Evacuate. Evacuate . . ."

"We'll all die," said Eddie. "But there's no point. You've lost. Go home."

"I don't lose," Shannon snarled.

"You should get used to it. I put the whole experiment out on the Internet fifteen minutes ago. All of it. The way Bucky wanted it."

Shannon laughed. "You think it matters? You think anyone else wants their economy destroyed? You think Japan or Germany or Korea is going to be any different than we are? I already told you about the Middle East . . . Eddie, it'll disappear no matter where you sent it."

"I sent it to Honda," said Eddie, with a thin smile. "I sent it to Ford, Chrysler, GM. I sent it to Mitsubishi and Mercedes and Microsoft, KIA, IBM. I sent it to Apple and Intel. I sent it to Allied and Gentech. I sent it to every multinational I could think of. And then I nailed the formula to a homepage, so if I forgot anyone they'll know where to find it . . . And you, Shannon, you were worried about lines on a map? That's dinosaur thinking, Shannon."

"How could you post that? That computer had no outside link."

"Come on," said Eddie. "How much trouble do you think I'd have building a modem?"

Shannon looked at his young nemesis for a long time. He had been beaten and he knew it. He acknowledged it with a nod.

"I guess I've been working for the wrong people." His eyes left Eddie's face and looked beyond him. Butler was hopping down the corridor as fast as he could. Shannon turned away in disgust.

At that moment all the main lights in the complex died. A second later the emergency lights came on. The tunnels filled with a harsh glare and long shadows. Shannon was nowhere to be seen—but that did not surprise Eddie in the least.

"Explosive atmosphere at seventeen per cent," the PA announced. "Air conditioning shutdown. Switching to twelve volt backup."

Holding a huge emergency flashlight, Collier rushed through a set of older tunnels, old civil defense signs on the walls. There were footsteps and he swung around, catching Shannon in the glare of the lamp.

"Get that out of my eyes," he said, slamming a pressure door behind him. Shannon pushed past Collier and opened the next pressure door. "Hurry up, Collier."

Then suddenly Shannon was struck with a desire too strong to be denied. He slammed the heavy metal door and dropped the pin, locking it.

Collier screamed through the wire glass inset. "What are you doing?"

"I said hurry," said Shannon. "You weren't fast enough."

Shannon was no fool. In the back of his mind, he had sensed that this day might come, so he had worked out an escape plan in advance. The Civil Defense bomb shelter ran deep into the rock of the mountain, a roughhewn corridor which ran directly to a single door. It was made of high-density tempered titanium steel, thousands and thousands of sheets of it until the twenty-foot-high door was a full foot and a half thick and weighed two and a half tons. Despite its weight, though, the door was so perfectly weighted and counterbalanced it opened easily.

Shannon darted into his private bomb shelter, as good a place as any to pass the Apocalypse.

Eddie and Lily were going out the way he had come in. He led her through the drainage tunnel, the two of them splashing through the water, going with the current this time. They were moving fast, but the rushing flow cut their legs out from underneath them, and they fell and slid against the rough concrete.

Down in the lab, hydrogen was being generated at such a rate that the gas was beginning to blow through the corridors, howling like a hurricane. The gale penetrated into the drainage system and thrust Eddie and Lily along even faster, smashing them through the hole and into the upper tunnel.

The pump was still there chattering away, but being overwhelmed by the force of the water and the wind.

Lily looked right and left, the tunnel dark at both ends. "Which way?"

Eddie was momentarily at a loss. He looked to the numbers spray-painted on the wall and pointed. "If the numbers are going down, it's that way." Hand-in-hand they ran, charging through the shaft that roared with the hydrogen wind.

Deep down below them, Butler lay sprawled in front of one of the elevators, his chest heaving. He couldn't climb the emergency stairs—he didn't have the strength, and all electrical systems had shut down. The wind carried the edge of the Rolling Stones song along with it. It would be the last thing he would hear.

Collier couldn't even hear that. He was trapped between the two pressure doors, running from one to the other, pounding frantically. Then he slid down the wall and put his hands over his head, making himself as small as possible, rocking gently, whimpering and waiting for the end.

In the laboratory the last strains of the last song on the tape died away, the capstans gathered up the last of the feeder, and the machine snapped off. That small mechanical movement generated the tiniest of blue electric arcs.

The ignition of the millions of cubic feet of hydrogen gas was made all the more terrible by the sturdiness of the space in which it was confined. The gas could not blast through the concrete and tons of mountain rock, so it was forced to follow the channels made by the dozens of corridors. The fireballs raced through the passageways, filling them with white-hot flame, incinerating everything in their vengeful path.

The heat was so intense that the metal supports and rebar melted inside the walls, the concrete slagging off like wax off a candle. The underground complex was imploding with the concentration of the blast.

A tongue of blue flame shot straight up the elevator shaft, blowing apart the building that concealed it, throwing bricks and masonry into the sky as if blown from the crater of a volcano. The ground trembled, and the FBI men and the survivors gathered at the top were thrown to the ground.

The explosions deep underground thundered and rolled like a summer storm. The air was electric, charged with the residue of superheated gas.

Ford staggered to his feet and stumbled a few yards. Smoke was now pouring from the various excavations as if from old-fashioned factory chimneys. There was no sign of Eddie or Lily.

Then from below came a sound, a deep, rumbling gurgling sound, as if the entire mountain was about to vomit up the fire. And a second later a great geyser of water and debris blasted from the secondary tunnel, carrying with it a small dumpster containing Eddie and Lily. They bailed out, hit the ground, and rolled as the pressure wave shot hundreds of feet into the sky.

Eddie and Lily lay on the muddy ground, stunned, beaten, not quite able to believe that they were actually alive. Then Lily rolled over and kissed Eddie full on the lips and hard. He was surprised, to say the least, but he didn't mind at all.

When they broke the clinch Eddie looked up to see a man standing over them, the light behind him, his face in shadows.

"Eddie Kasalivich?"

"Agent Ford?"

Ford stretched out a hand and helped Lily and Eddie to their feet. "So Eddie, you guilty of anything I should know about?"

"No," said Eddie.

"I didn't think so. Hey, Seamus, you owe me a hundred bucks. No checks."

Deep down, in the wreckage of the lab and the rest of the complex, James Shannon's private bomb shelter had withstood the explosion of the hydrogen. He waited until a few minutes after the last explosion had rumbled away, then he pushed open the huge door and made his way through the rubble and dust of the devastated underground compound. The loss of the hydrogen lab was bad—but it was not the end of the world. After all, there was always room in the greater world for a man of his peculiar talents. If Eddie had sent the formula to the industrial giants, then that was where James Shannon would go. The multinationals were always hiring.

He climbed toward the light, trailing sweet cigar smoke in his wake.

They were called the class from Hell—thirty-four inner-city sophomores she inherited from a teacher who'd been "pushed over the edge." She was told "those kids have tasted blood. They're dangerous."

But LouAnne Johnson had a different idea. Where the school system saw thirty-four unreachable kids, she saw young men and women with intelligence and dreams. When others gave up on them, she broke the rules to give them the best things a teacher can give— hope and belief in themselves. When statistics showed the chances were they'd never graduate, she fought to beat the odds.

This is her remarkable true story—and theirs.

DANGEROUS MINDS

LOUANNE JOHNSON

NOW A MAJOR MOTION PICTURE FROM HOLLYWOOD PICTURES STARRING

MICHELLE PFEIFFER

Alcatraz. The prison fortress off the coast of San Francisco. No man had gotten out alive before his time was up, until a 20-year-old petty thief named Willie Moore broke out.

Recaptured, then thrown into a pitch-black hellhole for three agonizing years, Willie is driven to near-madness—and finally to a brutal killing. Now, up on first-degree murder charges, he must wrestle with his nightmares and forge an alliance with Henry Davidson, the embattled lawyer who will risk losing his career and the woman he loves in a desperate bid to save Willie from the gas chamber.

Together, Willie and Henry will dare the most impossible act of all: get Willie off on a savage crime that the system drove him to commit—and put Alcatraz itself on trial.

MURDER IN THE FIRST

Dan Gordon

NOW A MAJOR MOTION PICTURE STARRING CHRISTIAN SLATER, KEVIN BACON, AND GARY OLDMAN

He's already blown up a subway. He's already sent the NYPD scrambling. Now, he's holding the entire city of New York hostage with the world's deadliest explosive— and he's making John McClane jump through hoops.

Once McClane was the best. Then he lost everything. Now, he's racing against the clock, following orders from a psycho bomber who's made massive destruction into a very personal game of revenge: when the city goes up, McClane will die first.

It can't happen. It won't happen. With a tough, streetwise partner, John McClane races across a panicked city, smashing the rules, locked and loaded for the ultimate duel...

DIE HARD
WITH A VENGEANCE

A novel by D. Chiel
Based on a screenplay written by Jonathan Hensleigh
Now a major motion picture
Starring Bruce Willis, Jeremy Irons and Samuel L. Jackson
and Directed by John McTiernan

_____ 95676-2 $4.99 U.S./$5.99 Can.

The victim is found facedown in a plate of spaghetti. It's the first in a series of unspeakable crimes so depraved and twisted that even veteran city cops can't look at them. And each murder comes with a name: this one is gluttony.

Somerset doesn't want this case. The city's best homicide cop, he's just one week from retiring—a week he planned to spend training his replacement David Mills, a real pain-in-the-butt go-getter. But after the second murder, Somerset knows there's a madman out there, one promising to avenge all seven deadly sins—and only he and Mills can stop him....

SEVEN

THE ELECTRIFYING NOVEL
BY ANTHONY BRUNO—
BASED ON THE BLOCKBUSTER MOTION PICTURE
STARRING BRAD PITT AND MORGAN FREEMAN